GOODBYE STRANGER

GOODBYE STRANGER

REBECCA STEAD

WENDY
LAMB
BOOKS

Text copyright © 2015 by Rebecca Stead
Jacket art copyright © 2015 by Marcos Chin

All rights reserved. Published in the United States by Wendy Lamb Books, an imprint of Random House Children's Books, a division of Penguin Random House LLC, New York.

Wendy Lamb Books and the colophon are trademarks of Penguin Random House LLC.

Visit us on the Web! randomhousekids.com

Educators and librarians, for a variety of teaching tools, visit us at RHTeachersLibrarians.com

Library of Congress Cataloging-in-Publication Data
Stead, Rebecca.
    Goodbye stranger / Rebecca Stead. — First edition.
        pages cm
    ISBN 978-0-385-74317-4 (trade) — ISBN 978-0-375-99098-4 (lib. bdg.) — ISBN 978-0-307-98085-4 (ebook) — ISBN 978-0-307-98086-1 (pbk.) [1. Best friends—Fiction. 2. Friendship—Fiction. 3. Middle schools—Fiction. 4. Schools—Fiction. 5. Family life—New York (State)—New York—Fiction. 6. New York (N.Y.)—Fiction.]
I. Title.
    PZ7.S80857Goo 2015
    [Fic]—dc23
                                    2014037289

The text of this book is set in 11.8-point Goudy.
Jacket design by Kate Gartner and Katrina Damkoehler
Interior design by Stephanie Moss

Printed in the United States of America
10 9 8 7 6 5
First Edition

For my friends,
including the one I married

GOODBYE STRANGER

PROLOGUE

When she was eight years old, Bridget Barsamian woke up in a hospital, where a doctor told her she shouldn't be alive. It's possible that he was complimenting her heart's determination to keep pumping when half her blood was still uptown on 114th Street, but more likely he was scolding her for roller-skating into traffic the way she had.

Despite what it looked like, she *had* been paying attention—she saw the red light ahead, and the cars. She merely failed to realize how quickly she was approaching them. Her skates had a way of making her feel powerful and relaxed, and it was easy to lose track of her speed.

When she was eight, Bridget loved two things: Charlie Chaplin and VW Bugs. She practiced her Chaplin moves whenever she could—his funny duckwalk and the casually choppy way he zoomed around on his skates, arms straight down, legs swinging.

Her interest in Volkswagen Bugs was less aesthetic. Whenever she saw one, she shouted, "Bug-buggy, ZOO-buggy!" which entitled her to punch whoever she happened to be with, twice, on the arm.

She saw the red light and the traffic that afternoon, but

she also saw a yellow VW Bug double-parked near a fire hydrant. So, still hurtling toward Broadway, she turned her head to yell "Bug-buggy, ZOO-buggy!" at her friend Tabitha, who was on a scooter right behind her. She wanted to be sure Tabitha heard her loud and clear, because she intended to hit her on the arm, twice, when they stopped at the corner, and didn't want any arguments.

"Bug-buggy, ZOO-buggy!" she shouted.

But Tabitha had fallen behind. "WHAT?" Tabitha called back.

So Bridget started again. "BUG—" And she flew straight past the corner into the street, a Chaplin move if there ever was one, accompanied by the high music of two screaming mothers—her own and Tabitha's—from somewhere far behind.

She missed third grade, but her body repaired itself. After four surgeries and a year of physical therapy, she showed no sign of injury. But Bridget was different, after: she froze sometimes when she was about to cross the street, both legs locked against her will, and she had a recurring nightmare that she'd been wrapped head to toe like a mummy, from which she always woke with a sucking breath, kicking at her covers.

The nightmares began when she was still in the hospital. In those days, which stretched into weeks, her mother sometimes brought her cello and played quietly at the foot of Bridget's bed. Sometimes her mother's music drew designs behind Bridget's closed eyelids. Sometimes it put her to sleep. One afternoon, Bridge woke to the sound of her mother's cello and said loudly, "I want to be called Bridge after this. I don't feel like Bridget anymore." Still playing, her mother nodded, and Bridge went back to sleep.

There was one other thing. On the day Bridge was discharged from the hospital, one of the nurses said something that changed the way she thought about herself. The nurse said, "Thirteen broken bones and a punctured lung. You must have been put on this earth for a reason, little girl, to have survived."

It was a nicer, more interesting way of saying what the doctor had told her when she first woke up after the accident. Bridge couldn't answer the nurse, because by that time her jaw had been wired shut. Otherwise, she might have asked, "What *is* the reason?" Instead, the question stayed in her head, where it circled.

THE CAT EARS

Bridge started wearing the cat ears in September, on the third Monday of seventh grade.

The cat ears were black, on a black headband. Not exactly the color of her hair, but close. Checking her reflection in the back of her cereal spoon, she thought they looked surprisingly natural.

On the table in front of her was a wrinkled sheet of homework. It wasn't homework yet, actually. Aside from her name, the paper was blank. She itched to draw a small, round Martian in the upper left-hand corner.

Instead, she put down the spoon, picked up her pen, and wrote:

What is love?

This was her assignment: answer the question "What is love?"

In full sentences.

She looked at the empty blue lines on the page and tried to imagine them full of words.

Love is _____.

Her mom had once told her that love was a kind of music. One day, you could just . . . hear it.

"Was it like that when you met Dad?" Bridge had asked. "Like hearing music for the first time?"

"Oh, I heard the music before that," her mom had said. "And I danced with a few people before I met Daddy. But when I found him, I knew I had a dance partner for life."

But Bridge couldn't write that. And anyway, her mom was a cellist. Everything was about music to her.

Bridge squeezed her eyes closed until she saw glittery things floating in the dark. Then she started writing, quickly.

Love is when you like someone so much that you can't just call it "like," so you have to call it "love."

It was only one sentence, but she was out of time.

Bridge had noticed the cat ears earlier that morning, on the shelf above her desk, where they'd been sitting since the previous Halloween. They felt strange at first, and made the sides of her head throb a tiny bit when she chewed her cereal, but as she walked toward school, the ears became a comforting presence. When she was small, her father would sometimes rest his hand on her head as they went down the street. It was a little bit like that.

Bridge stopped just outside the front doors of her school, slipped her phone out of her pocket, and texted her mom:

At school.

XOXO, her mom texted back.

Bridge's mother was on an Amtrak train, coming home from a performance in Boston with her string quartet. Bridge's father, who owned a coffee place a few blocks from their apartment, had to be at the store by seven a.m. And her brother, Jamie, left early for high school. His subway ride was almost an hour long.

So there had been no one at home that morning to make her think twice about the cat ears. Not that anyone in her family was the type to try to stop her from wearing them in the first place. And not that she was the type to *be* stopped.

Tabitha was next to Bridge's locker, waiting. "Hurry up, the bell's about to ring."

"Okay." Bridge faced her locker and puckered up. "One, two . . ." She leaned in and kissed the skinny metal door.

"Nice one. You can stop doing that anytime, you know."

Bridge spun her lock and jerked the door open. "Not until the end of the month." Seventh grade was the year they finally got to have lockers, and Bridge swore she was going to kiss hers every day until the end of September.

"You have ears," Tab said. "Extra ones, I mean."

"Yeah." Bridge put both hands up and touched the rounded tips of her cat ears. "Soft."

"They're sweet. You gonna wear them all day?"

"Maybe." Madame Lawrence might make her take them off, she knew. But Bridge didn't have French on Mondays.

If she had French on Mondays, life would really be unfair.

The next day she wore them again.

"*Un chat!*" Madame Lawrence said, pointing as Bridge took her seat at the very back of the room. And Bridge's head tingled in the way that happens when someone points. But that was all.

By Wednesday, the ears felt like a regular part of her.

VALENTINE'S DAY

You paint your toenails. You don't steal nail polish, though.

Vinny calls you chicken: all of her polish comes from the six-dollar manicure place. Every month, she puts another bottle in her pocket while the lady is getting the warm towel for her hands. You told her you want to be a lawyer and can't be stealing stuff. Vinny rolled her eyes. Then Zoe rolled *her* eyes. Vinny's eye-rolls are perfect dives, but Zoe always tries too hard. Her lids tremble and her eyeballs look like they might disappear into her head.

Your mother is shouting that it's time to leave for school. You suck in air and shout back: "Just a minute!" You are not going to school. She doesn't realize that, of course.

It turns out that, in high school, not painting your toenails is considered disgusting. You blow on your wet toes, little puffs. "So much for the freshman-year perfect-attendance certificate," you tell yourself.

"What?" Your mother is standing in the doorway looking impatient.

"Nothing," you say.

She squeaks about your flip-flops, how it's February, but

you tell her it's fine, it's not so cold, there's no gym today, and nobody cares.

Really you are just going to hang out in the park until she leaves for work. Then you will come back home.

Your feet are ice. The flip-flops were a stupid idea—what were you thinking? The playground swings are freezing and your hands ache, but you hold on, walk yourself back a few steps, and let your body fly.

It feels wonderful.

The playground is deserted. It's too early for little kids to be out, especially in February, and everyone else is where you're supposed to be: at school. On your way to the park, you had to dodge Bridge Barsamian, struggling with a big cardboard box, those tatty-looking cat ears she's been wearing since September peeking over the top. You sidestepped into a bodega just in time.

You lean forward and swing back, lean back and swing forward.

Straight ahead of you is the big rock where you played when you were little. There's a divot in it, a crater where everyone dumped acorns, leaves, grass, those poison red berries if there were any. You poured them from your shirt-hammocks into the crater and poked the mess with sticks. "Dinner!" You'd all sit in a circle, and Vinny would dare everyone to lick their berry-stained fingers. She was always in charge—even then, before you understood it, her beauty was hard to look away from: glossy dark hair and full red lips. Snow White with a tan and a strut.

. . .

It's windy on the little platform at the top of the wooden climbing tower. The short walls are covered with messages scrawled in thick marker, big sloppy hearts and dirty words. When you were small, you would swing yourself up legs-first, but now you have to stick your head through the opening in the floor and then hoist the rest. You certainly have grown, you tell yourself.

You sit on the rough plank floor and wedge your back into the nearest corner, the one that was always yours. You can almost see them, in their places: Vinny to the left, Zoe to the right. They're not your friends anymore. They're both other people now. The girls you can see looking back at you are gone. No one talks about these disappearances. Everyone pretends it's all right.

Remember the time you found a beer bottle up here? It was empty, but the three of you took turns holding it, staggering around and pretending to drink—though never touching it to your lips; that would have been disgusting. You felt almost drunk for real.

Vinny's father had been there that afternoon, seen you, and demanded that you all come down. He took the empty bottle with one hand and jerked Vinny's arm with the other, dragging her toward a garbage can. She tried to cover, acting like she was just walking along next to him, double-time.

You check your phone. Your mom was getting into the shower when you left. You wonder if she has left for work.

You can see the sun touching the tops of the buildings

12

across the street, making its way through the neighborhood like someone whose attention you are careful not to attract. It's still shady in the playground. But aside from the loneliness, and the cold, it's all exactly the same. If you keep your own body out of sight, you could be nine years old again.

ANOTHER BOOK ON TOP

When Bridge came back to school in fourth grade, after the accident, Tabitha introduced her to Emily. And then Tab and Emily showed Bridge how they drew little animals on their homework, in the upper left-hand corners of their papers, underneath their names. Tab always drew a funny bird, and Emily always drew a spotted snake.

They said that Bridge should choose an animal to draw in the upper left-hand corners of *her* homework, and then they would be a club.

Bridge announced that she was allergic to clubs, that she would rather be a *set*, like in math. Her mother had homeschooled her. Actually, a lot of it had been hospital school.

"A set?" Tab repeated.

"Yes," Bridge said. "We could be the set of all fourth graders who draw animals on their homework papers."

That night, Bridge thought about what her animal should be. A cat? A frog? She decided she would draw a Martian, with a circle body, a circle mouth, two feet but no legs, and three eyes.

The next day, she showed her Martian to Tab and Emily,

feeling shy. But Tab clapped when she saw it, and Emily said "Awesome!" And then the three of them held up their papers in a kind of circle on the lunch table, so that their animals could see one another.

"Is a Martian an animal, though?" Bridge asked.

"A Martian is a *creature*," Tab said. "And so is a snake. And so is a bird."

And from then on, they were the set of all fourth graders who drew creatures on their homework. More than that, they were friends.

The next year, Bridge, Tab, and Emily were the set of fifth graders who drew creatures on their homework papers, and they drew the same things they had drawn before: bird, snake, and Martian. Their friendship grew stronger, like a rope that thickened little by little. On the Monday after spring vacation, Emily sighed, rested her chin on the lunchroom table, and said, "Can sets have rules?"

"Sure," Bridge said.

"What rules?" Tab asked, suspicious.

"It's only one rule," Em said. "No fighting."

"No fighting?" Bridge said.

"Yeah, just—no fighting. Okay?"

"But we have to swear on something," Tab said. She put her second Twinkie in the middle of the table. "Let's swear on this."

Em smiled. "The magic Twinkie of no fighting?"

They each ate a third.

When middle school started, they were the set of sixth graders who drew creatures on their homework and did not fight. That was the year Em's parents got divorced. The rope became even stronger.

In seventh grade, things were different. Not the rope. Other things.

First of all, now Emily had a "body." Bridge could see this for herself, and Tab's older sister, Celeste, who was in high school, confirmed it:

"Look at Emily with the curvy new curves!"

It had happened quickly. Bridge heard her mother telling her father that Emily's "growth spurt" made her think of those silent four-year-olds who suddenly start speaking in full sentences.

Seventh grade had sports teams and foreign languages. Emily turned out to be not only the second-fastest runner in the grade but also one of the best players on the girls' JV soccer team, and now even the eighth graders said hi to her. And Tab, who had always spoken French at home but almost never raised her hand at school, became kind of a know-it-all. Madame Lawrence, who was very strict, sometimes chatted and laughed with Tab before class. In French.

Bridge was horrible at French.

And then Bridge's English teacher handed back the first homework assignment of the year. He had circled her three-eyed Martian and written *No doodling on homework, please. Next time I will take off points.*

When she showed Emily and Tab and asked if anyone had drawn big red circles around *their* creatures, they looked at each other and admitted that they hadn't drawn anything on their homework in the first place.

"You guys." Bridge dropped her arm so that her paper slapped her thigh. "Seriously?"

Emily grabbed Bridge's hand and said, "We're still a set. We're the set of all seventh graders who *used* to draw stuff on their homework."

"And who don't fight," Tab added. "Don't forget the Twinkie."

"Right," Em said. She looked at Bridge. "Forever."

"And ever," Tab said.

But Bridge understood that life didn't balance anymore. Life was a too-tall stack of books that had started to lean to one side, and each new day was another book on top.

MAYBE

Emily had long legs, and her chest jiggled a little when she moved. She probably jiggled exactly the right amount. And it didn't slow her down on the soccer field. At all.

"Wow, she just *exploded*," Bridge heard someone say after Em scored a goal during the first game of the season. But she wasn't sure if it was Emily's speed or her body that was exploding. She and Tab watched the kids running back and forth in the knee-high dust. It was almost October but still summer-hot.

"So what's with the ears?" Tab asked.

Bridge shrugged. "They're ears."

"It's been a week. How long are you going to wear them?"

"I don't know." Bridge could feel Tab studying her, but she didn't turn her head. "Maybe until it rains?" She touched the cat ears carefully with four fingers. "I don't want them to get wet."

"Are you okay?" Tab asked.

"Sure," Bridge said.

On the last day of September, Bridge kissed her locker for the last time and Emily got a text from a boy. It had not rained. Bridge was still wearing the ears.

The text was from an eighth grader. It said: S'up?

"Wild," Em said.

"Are you gonna text him back?" Tab asked.

"Maybe," Emily said.

On the first day of October, Emily got a text from a boy asking for a picture.

"Same boy," Em said. "That eighth grader. His name is Patrick. Very cute, actually. And he plays soccer." They were sitting against the fence after Emily's second win.

"A picture of what?" Tab asked, pulling at the dry grass. She was stirring up dust that made Bridge want to sneeze.

Emily laughed. "It doesn't matter. I'm not doing it."

"Send him a picture of your feet," Bridge suggested.

And so Emily took a picture of her dirt-covered soccer cleats and texted it to Patrick.

Ten seconds later, he texted Emily a picture of *his* sneakers.

"Ha," Emily said, shoving her phone into her bag. "He thinks he's funny."

VALENTINE'S DAY

You should have known about Vinny. You *did* know. You'd known ever since that day last fall, when it was the three of you, playing one of Vinny's games. You watched her blindfold Zoe, who sat obediently on your kitchen floor while Vinny quietly cut a slice from a banana, giggling and telling you to shush. She fed the banana slice to Zoe with a spoon, saying, "Don't peek! Don't peek!"

Then it was your turn. You sat smiling on the floor, blindfolded with a pair of your own black tights, and Vinny came with her spoon, laughing. "Open wide!"

It was a spoonful of pure cinnamon. You choked and ran to the bathroom to spit and spit and spit into the sink before you came out, smiling again, eyes watering. Ha. No big deal. At dinner that night your sister asked you three times what was wrong. *Nothing,* you said. *Nothing.* Until your mom told her you were just being a teenager.

A week later, you asked Gina if she felt like hanging out. She hadn't gone to your middle school, and her sense of humor made geometry bearable.

Big mistake. Vinny's eyes feasted on Gina's clothes, her sneakers, her lack of purse. As soon as the four of you were in your room, Vinny clapped her hands and called out, "Tasting game!"

This time you got the banana. And then you watched Vinny feed Gina a spoonful of black pepper. She couldn't stop coughing and had to go home, apologizing.

Gina was the one who apologized.

You were the one who let it happen.

You can't stand this freezing-cold playground for another minute. Your mom must have left for work by now. You want your bed. You want to lie down and disappear. But first you have to get home: six blocks. You don't want to have to explain yourself to anyone, especially anyone who might see your parents later. You tell yourself that it'll be like a game of hot lava. Vinny used to love that game when you were little. She'd shout, "The floor is lava!" and leap from your couch to your coffee table to the chair your dad had shipped all the way from Paris because he said it was the most comfortable thing in the world. No one jumped on the furniture at Vinny's house.

Your old middle school is hot lava.

Zoe's nosy doorman is hot lava.

The Bean Bar is hot lava.

You cross Broadway and rush past the Dollar-Eight Diner, where the waitress still calls you French Fry because when you were little that was all you would eat.

You get to your building and decide that the elevator is hot lava, so you take the stairs.

Breathing hard, you put your ear against the apartment door and listen for a few seconds, just in case.

Key in the lock, turn, and push. You're in.

There's no one home. You go straight to your room, shut the door, and stand looking at the bed you made two hours ago, when the apartment was full of voices and the smell of toast and news on the radio and the wet warmth that floated out from the hall bathroom where your sister had showered for too long.

You put your feet in the middle of the rug. You lie down neatly on your bed.

The whole world is hot lava.

TEN THOUSAND STEPS

Madame Lawrence spoke only French in class. On the first day, Bridge raised her hand and said, "Excuse me, but we don't understand anything you're saying. We don't speak French yet." She smiled, a little embarrassed for Madame Lawrence, who'd missed something so obvious.

"*En Français, s'il vous plaît,*" Madame Lawrence said gently.

"What?" Bridge said.

"She wants you to say it in French," Tab told Bridge quietly over her shoulder. She sat three rows ahead.

"How can I say it in French if I don't speak French?" Bridge said in English. "If I knew French, I wouldn't be taking French to begin with."

She was careful not to look at Tab when she said this.

"*En Français,*" Madame Lawrence said, a little less gently.

The words didn't come in French. When she tried to speak in French, Bridge felt as if someone had sewn her mouth closed, which made her angry. And when she was angry she couldn't learn because there were too many angry words in her head. So the French homework wasn't so easy either.

• • •

At Emily's third soccer game, Bridge and Tab stood together in a drizzling rain.

"You're still wearing the ears," Tab said.

"I decided to wear them until Halloween," Bridge said.

After the game, Bridge bought two Kit Kats, one of which she dropped on her father's desk at the Bean Bar on her way home. He was out, but he'd know the Kit Kat was from her.

There was a new girl behind the counter. She didn't seem at all curious about why Bridge felt free to walk into the tiny office next to the bathrooms.

"Hi," Bridge said on her way out.

"Hi," the girl said. "I'm Adrienne." She held out her hand, and Bridge reached out to shake.

"You work here," Bridge said.

"Yes," Adrienne agreed.

Bridge blushed. "I meant—"

"Are you Bridge, by any chance? You look like your dad."

"Thanks." Bridge realized how that sounded, blushed again. "I mean—"

Adrienne smiled. "No, that's right. It was a compliment. He's super-cute, as far as dads go. You should see *my* dad. What is he, anyway, an Arab?"

"He's Armenian. Armenian American."

"Armenian?" She nodded. "Cool. I don't even know where that is."

"Well, he was born in California," Bridge said. "What happened to Mark?"

"Beats me," Adrienne said. "I guess he quit. My lucky day."

• • •

"Mark quit the Bean Bar," Bridge told her brother, Jamie, when she got home.

"Yeah, bummer." Jamie was sitting on the edge of his bed, fiddling with something on his wrist. "I liked Mark. He always gave me a doughnut. A *first-day* doughnut." Their dad was more generous with the day-old baked goods.

"There's a new one," Bridge said. "Adrienne."

"I know." The thing he was fiddling with began to beep.

"What is that?"

"A pedometer. It counts your steps."

"What for?"

"A contest."

"Seriously? Another one?"

Jamie met Bridge's eyes. "I'm going to beat him this time."

Him was Alex, who lived on the top floor of their building. He was in tenth grade, like Jamie, and they were sort of friends, sort of enemies. "Frenemies," Em called it.

"Nah," Jamie said when Bridge told him that. "Frenemies is a middle-school thing."

"Okay, so what do you call it in high school?"

"I guess now he's my . . ." Jamie thought, and then smiled. "He's my nemesis."

Alex was always suggesting some kind of competition, and Jamie was always losing. So far he'd forfeited a brand-new *Call of Duty* game, a vintage Rolling Stones T-shirt he'd bought at the flea market, and a baseball signed by Mariano Rivera. Bridge wondered what Jamie had left that Alex would even want. She scanned her brother's room: books, old art projects, a few binders of ordinary baseball cards, and his action figure of Hermey the elf. Jamie wouldn't bet his laptop, would he? Their parents would lose their minds.

"So what's the contest?" she said.

"Alex and I are going to walk ten thousand steps every day. *Exactly* ten thousand steps." He tapped his wrist. "This thingy counts every step, and then at midnight it downloads so we can check each other's numbers. First one who goes over or under ten thousand loses."

"What'd you bet him this time?"

"It doesn't matter. Because I'm not going to lose."

"Mom and Dad won't let you bet your laptop."

"I didn't bet my laptop."

"Not Hermey!" She grabbed the plastic elf from Jamie's bookcase and rubbed his yellow hair protectively. He was a character from the Rudolph Christmas special. They watched it every year. Rudolph was a reindeer misfit because of his glowing red nose, and Hermey was an elf misfit because he didn't like making toys. He wanted to be a dentist.

Jamie smiled. "I would never let Alex have Hermey."

"So what'd you bet?" Bridge said, walking Hermey's pointy boots along the edge of Jamie's bed.

"I told you. It doesn't matter."

Bridge didn't have to ask what Jamie was trying to win back from Alex. She knew it was the Rolling Stones T-shirt.

DEMENTED

Emily was leaning against her locker and smiling at her phone.

"What's funny?" Bridge asked.

"More texts," Emily said, holding out her phone.

Tab snatched it. "Ew. What is that?"

Emily grabbed the phone back and studied the screen. "It's not *ew*," she said. "It's a knee."

"*Whose* knee?"

"Somebody's."

"That eighth grader?"

"His name is Patrick. And it turns out half of JV soccer is in love with him."

"Even the boys?" Tab said.

"Probably," Em said.

"Are you wearing eye makeup?" Bridge said.

"A little," Em admitted. "What do you think?"

Bridge tilted her head. "I don't know yet. I have to get used to it."

"Wait, look." Em waved her phone at them. "*This* one's cute. I promise."

"What is that?" Tab asked. "Your elbow?"

"No, doofus!" Em's voice dropped. "It's his ankle. Cute, right?"

Bridge rotated the phone, trying to make out an ankle. "Why did he send you a picture of his ankle? And his knee?"

"Because! Remember? My foot?"

"So you sent him a picture of your foot and he sent you one of his ankle?"

"Yeah." Em smiled.

"The set of all people who send pictures of their leg parts," Bridge said.

"Yeah."

"I'm guessing it's a small set. Maybe just the two of you."

"A set of two," Em said.

"Get that dreamy look off your face," Tab said. "You're being . . . manipulated!"

"I am not!"

"Let me guess. Now he wants a picture of *your* knee, right?"

"So?"

"The Berperson says that women are treated like objects and we don't even know it."

"The Berperson! Give me a break. She's a wacko."

"She is not!"

The Berperson was Tab's English teacher. Her name was Ms. Berman, but on the first day of school she had instructed the class that this year they were going to be detectives, looking for the "hidden messages" in language. Then she had written her own name on the board, crossed out the *man*, and written *person* over it. "Call me Ms. Berperson!" she said. But everyone called her the Berperson instead.

Em used her thumb to flip back and forth between her Patrick photos: ankle, knee, ankle, knee. "Seriously, you guys, what should I send back? Should I do, like, my shin?" She hesitated. "That might be really ugly."

"Why don't you and Patrick actually *talk* to each other?" Tab said.

Em looked up. "Are you demented? And say what?"

VALENTINE'S DAY

You gather up the cat and try to make her snuggle the way she does early in the morning, when she purrs like a lawn mower and rubs the side of her face against your cheek. But she's having none of it and hops off the bed.

You put your headphones on and pull your sweatshirt hood up over them.

Head hug, you think. It's something Gina does—squeezes your head to her body with one arm, yells "Head hug!" and then cracks up.

You listen to one of your mom's old French songs—she's always loading her music onto your playlist by accident. You pretend to mind, but don't. Her songs remind you of being little, when she played them loud and said how they were about life going by too fast.

Life was anything but fast, in your opinion. If it went any more slowly, time would probably start to run backward.

You walk around the house with your hood pulled tight and stop in front of your dad's cactuses. *Cacti*. They look soft and fuzzy, but you know if you touch them, tiny spikes will get stuck in your fingers, hurt like crazy, and be impossible to get out. So you just look at them, standing with your hands in your hoodie pockets.

The phone scares the heck out of you. You don't answer it. After five rings, the machine picks up. It's the school. A recording.

"This is a reminder that when your child is going to be absent from high school, a call is required by nine a.m. . . ."

Oh *no*. Will school call your mom or dad at work? If so, they'll both come running. Correction: they'll try your cell, they'll freak completely out, they'll imagine that you're dead in a ditch, and then they'll come running.

You don't want them to come running. You want a day alone. One day.

But you don't want them to think you're dead in a ditch.

Do they even have ditches in New York City?

Suddenly you want something to eat. Toast, you think.

Your cell phone rings before you can get the bread out of the bag. You look without touching while it vibrates on the kitchen counter: your mom's work number. You drop two slices into the toaster and let it go to voice mail.

As soon as your cell goes quiet, the house phone rings. You listen to your mom's voice on the machine. She says your name and sounds worried. Listening, you reflect that you are probably the worst person on the planet. But this is not exactly news.

Your mom's office is all the way downtown, forty minutes away at least, and your dad's is even farther. You figure you have a little time. Then you'll have to go somewhere. You'll text one of them, though. To say you aren't in a ditch.

Sixty seconds later, someone is knocking at the door. Your brain slows down as your heart rocks out through your ears.

31

Then a voice is calling your name. You recognize it: your neighbor. The one who feeds the cat when your family's away. Your mom must have called her.

The doorknob rattles. Good thing you locked the door. You stand perfectly still on the old floorboards. One good squeak could give you away.

Your toast pops, and your head snaps toward it as if there might be a sniper in the pantry. Stay calm, you tell yourself: she'll go back to her apartment in a second. You'll butter your toast and make a plan.

Then you hear it—the sound of a key in the lock.

She has keys!

You sprint toward your room, think again, and pivot on one foot.

You know where to hide.

HUMAN ON THE MOON

Bridge's first English assignment of the year had been a one-page essay about "something of interest." And now, weeks later, they all had to "exchange papers with a neighbor" for "peer editing," which was embarrassing.

She traded with Sherm Russo, who sat to her left, and watched his eyes go straight to the Martian with the red circle around it and the teacher's threat about taking off points.

Sherm's paper was about the supermoon. A supermoon, it said, was a full moon that comes closer than usual to Earth. Bridge had assumed that the moon was always the same distance from Earth. Didn't it go just around in a circle, like a ball on a string?

She put that question in the margin.

"Actually," Sherm said, reading over her shoulder, "it's an elliptical orbit. So sometimes it's closer and sometimes it's farther away."

"Oh, right," Bridge said. "I forgot." She erased her question, tilting her head so that her hair fell like a dark curtain between them.

"I like your Martian," Sherm said.

"Thanks." She pushed his paper across the desk. "Here you go. I can't really find any mistakes or anything."

"Oh." His neck turned pink. She looked at her paper and saw that he'd been busy marking it up. He had made some sort of correction on almost every line.

"Just some punctuation and stuff," he said, sliding it over to her.

"Can you believe this?" Bridge said at lunch. "He wrote all over it!"

"He did you a favor," Tab said, scanning the paper. "Your grammar needs work."

Em squinted through the cafeteria windows. "Crap. It's raining."

"I haven't even told you the dumbest part," Bridge said. "The dumbest part is that *then* he tells me that he doesn't believe anyone ever actually landed on the moon!"

"Oh, neither does my dad," Em said.

"Are you serious?"

Em nodded. "He says the government made it all up. But he might be joking. Sometimes I can't tell with my dad."

"What about Neil Armstrong?" Bridge said. "What about 'one small step for man, one giant leap for mankind'?"

Tab slapped the table. "Notice the 'man'? *Man*kind? Why didn't he say *human*kind?"

"There she goes again," Em said.

"I'm just saying," Tab said.

"Anyway," Em said, "my dad says that it was all bogus, probably filmed in a movie studio or something. I can't *believe* it's raining again. Smelly auditorium and *The Magic School Bus*. I hate *The Magic School Bus*."

"I love *The Magic School Bus,*" Tab said happily. "I hope it's the space one."

"Tab, it's for six-year-olds," Em said.

"Well, excuuuse me," Tab said.

Em rolled her eyes.

Bad weather meant no recess in the yard. Instead, the whole seventh grade sat in the auditorium and watched the same Magic School Bus cartoons over and over, except for the lucky homeroom that won the rock-paper-scissors tournament and escaped to the gym.

Bridge had been picked for the tournament once, at the end of sixth grade. Her legs shook the whole time she was up there, and she'd been relieved when she lost in the first round and could get off the stage.

This time her homeroom picked Emily, chanting "Em! Em! Em!"

Now that Bridge thought of it, it had been Em the last time, too.

Em ran down the aisle to the stage. Her legs were definitely not shaking. When she won her first game, she thrust both arms over her head as if she'd just been declared heavyweight champion of the world. When she made it to the final match, even kids in other classes were shouting "Go, Emily!" and everyone went berserk when she won. Em waved, did a goofy kind of jazz-hands thing, and then bounced off the stage and back to Bridge, who adjusted her ears and couldn't help feeling a little bit proud to be Em's friend. On their way out of the auditorium, they passed Tab on the end of a row.

"Woman power!" Tab shouted, pumping a fist in the air.

But when their class got to the gym, the maintenance guys were setting up tables around the edges of the room.

"For the clubs fair—sixth period," one explained. "You guys can sit in the middle if you're quiet."

"Sit in the middle?" Bridge said.

"Duck, duck, goose!" someone yelled.

"Lucky!" Tab said later, shoving her binder into her locker. "I love duck, duck, goose!"

"Well, you wouldn't have loved *this* duck, duck, goose." Bridge made a face. "It was idiotic. All the girls tapped boys and then just squealed like morons and barely even ran."

"Bridge, it was duck, duck, goose," Em said. "It's kind of dumb to begin with. And I'm wearing the wrong shoes. It's hard to run in these."

"Why do you wear high heels to school anyway?" Bridge said.

"These are not high heels! There's barely any heel. But the bottoms are slippery." Em lifted one foot to show them.

Bridge slammed her locker. "We should go, I guess. It's starting."

The clubs fair was mandatory for the whole seventh grade. When they walked into the gym, someone yelled "Emily!" and Em scanned the room, broke into a grin, and went straight to the soccer table, where she disappeared into a sea of matching yellow sweatshirts.

"I think I hate this," Bridge said, looking around.

"There are at least thirty different clubs here," Tab said. "Just pick something."

"I guess," Bridge said.

They waded into the crowd. "Everyone's walking clockwise," Tab said. "Let's go counterclockwise."

"What?" The noise was like a wave that kept getting bigger: two hundred seventh graders, all looking for someplace they belonged.

"This way!" Tab pointed left. She stopped almost immediately and gestured at the first table. "Chess?"

Bridge used to love chess. But she didn't want to join the Chess Club. She didn't want to join any club.

"This is dumb," she said.

"Come on!" Tab said. "You're being such a grouch!"

Bridge shrugged and adjusted her cat ears. Tab glanced at them and then looked at Bridge. "Let's keep going."

As they made their way around the room, Tab signed up for Hindi Club and French Club, where Madame Lawrence pointed at Bridge and said, *"Le chat!"*

Bridge pretended not to hear.

"Look!" Tab pointed at a table where a group of girls was gathered around a young woman with wavy hair and perfect makeup. "The Berperson!"

"That's the Berperson?" Bridge shouted over the roar. "I pictured someone old and short, with hair down to her knees."

Tab gave her a look. "Because only short, hairy people care about social justice?"

"No," Bridge said. "I think it's just the word 'Berperson.'"

"Come on, I want to introduce you," Tab said, dragging her by the arm. "Look—she runs the Human Rights Club! I didn't even know there was one!"

Tab hugged the Berperson. Bridge tried to imagine herself hugging her English teacher. Nope.

"This is my friend Bridge!" Tab yelled, pointing.

"Nice ears," the Berperson shouted. "As long as you're wearing them for yourself!"

Bridge didn't say anything. Who else would she be wearing them for?

Tab turned to her. "Let's join! This is so perfect!"

"I think I'll go all the way around first," Bridge said. "See what there is."

"You sure?" Now that she'd found the Berperson, Tab was clearly going no farther.

"Yeah," Bridge said, stepping away. "I'll come back."

Model UN. Spanish Club. Yearbook. No. No. No.

Current Events: no.

Bridge passed the sports clubs, where she saw Em sitting on the floor, looking at her phone, surrounded by girls in yellow sweatshirts looking at their phones. An eighth grader, Julie Hopper, had her legs across Em's lap. She was using a hole punch and a piece of loose-leaf paper to make confetti, which she occasionally threw at Em's ponytail. Some of it stuck there. Bridge kept moving.

Drama Club: no.

And then she came to the last few tables, which were quieter.

Robotics: no.

Photography: maybe.

She was almost back to the beginning of the circle. The last table was surrounded by a handful of seventh graders and a few older kids in black T-shirts.

"Hey there!" said the tallest black-T-shirt kid. "You interested in Tech Crew?"

Bridge took a step back. Hanging from the front of the table was a long banner that said MAKE MAGIC HAPPEN WITH TECH.

"Um," Bridge said. "I don't really know what it is."

"It's stagecraft—we do all the school shows. We make the sets, do the sound, the lighting. It's really cool. This is my second year. You should join. We need seventh graders."

That was when Bridge noticed Sherm Russo, not saying anything, behind the tall kid.

"Hi," she said.

He waved and stepped forward.

"You're doing this?" Bridge asked.

"Yeah. Seems cool. They build stuff and work at all the school shows and stuff." Sherm pointed at the tall kid. "He says they order pizza on show nights." He grinned.

"We do," the tall kid said, nodding. "The school pays for it. We have a budget, which is really rare. And Mr. Partridge is great. You shouldn't believe what people say about him."

"Uh, what do people say about him?" Bridge said.

The kid gave a funny wave. "Nothing. Just that he's mean. He's more, like, intense. Tech is kind of like a job, but a really cool job. We do the school play, the winter concert, the Valentine's Day show, everything."

Sherm looked at her. "You have to join something, right?"

That was true. She had to join something. It was a rule. "So what's it called again?" she asked the older kid. "Tech Club?"

"No, it's crew. Tech Crew." And he turned so that Bridge could see the word CREW in big block letters across the back of his black T-shirt.

Not a club.

Bridge smiled. "Where do I sign up?"

SHERM

October 7

Dear Nonno Gio,

I talked to Bridget Barsamian today. Remember her? It wasn't a big deal. We had to trade papers in English and ended up having a whole conversation. And then during clubs fair she walked right up to the Tech Crew table and joined. I definitely didn't think she was the Tech Crew type.

She wears these cat ears now, on a black headband. Kind of weird, kind of cute.

I'm getting your texts, but I just erase them. If you don't have an unlimited plan, you should save yourself the money.

From,
Sherm

P.S. There are four months and seven days until your birthday.

VALENTINE'S DAY

Your parents' closet makes you feel better right away. There's a dry smell and a feeling of protection. You find the small empty space you remember, behind your mom's long dresses hanging in their filmy dry-cleaner plastic. Your sister used to drag pillows back here and read by the light of her blue Star Wars light saber.

The neighbor lady won't check the closets, you tell yourself, but your body is a statue just in case. Even a hard exhale could move the dry-cleaner plastic and give you away.

You can't hear anything at all, which is interesting. At least, at first it's interesting. Then it's kind of great. And then it begins to weird you out.

Just *be*, you tell yourself. She'll leave soon.

Mom will be coming. Dad will be coming. If you want a day alone, you will obviously have to get out of the apartment. But first, you have to stay very still.

You stare into the dark and think about the stars at summer camp. Behind the actual stars, there's that *light* dusting the sky. Whenever you looked at that dust, you felt huge, as if you were part of everything.

Vinny sent letters and packages every summer. There was

a camp rule against junk food, so she'd wrap a bag of M&M's in brown paper, cover it with a thousand pieces of tape, and label it *thumbtacks* or something. Your counselors saw right through it but usually let you eat the candy.

Her letters always ended the same way: *Miss U, luv U, wouldn't want 2 B U!* Vinny's dad wouldn't let her go anywhere in the summer. She went to morning day camp and stayed in the apartment with her grandmother, mostly.

You spent hours writing back to Vinny all those summers, trying to make it sound as if the girls at camp were lame, as if you were hardly having fun at all. You left out your first-ever date, with a boy named Daniel who told you that you were beautiful and tie-dyed a T-shirt for you in the art barn. You left out Susannah, who lives in California and talked you into doing the play. You left out the lake, still your favorite place in the world. You left out late swim, at dusk, and the feeling you got every time you entered the glass-flat water that broke soft across your chin. You left out the way the trees bundled close and dark against the sky, and the wooden dock with the metal swimmer tags hanging on the pegboard that showed who was in the water and who was on dry land. Because you knew that, every single year, Vinny's heart broke a little when you left. And when Vinny got hurt, she got mean.

The narrow strip of light at the edge of the closet door widens, and your breath stops. But it's the cat, not the neighbor. Her eyes shine at you in the dark, and when you put one arm out, she lets you rub her between the eyes. Then a noise reaches you: somewhere, your cell phone is ringing. You realize you left it on the kitchen counter, next to the toaster. You hear the neighbor answer it.

"Hello?" She says it loudly. But after that, her voice drops.

You are very, very still. The cat is exploring your mother's shoes. You close your eyes and try to count the stars.

RAG ON A POLE

On Wednesdays and Fridays, Bridge woke to the sound of the cello. Her mom taught on those days and had to get in her practice hours early. Her music reminded Bridge of picking wildflowers—she started with something thin and simple and then kept adding new sounds, all different shapes and colors, until she had something explosive. But in the mornings her mom tried to explode very quietly, so that the people downstairs didn't get annoyed.

Most of the time, Bridge loved the music. Today, it made her feel heavy. It pinned her to her bed, and she had to wait for her mom to take a break before she could get herself up.

"Do you really think the moon landing was faked?" Bridge asked Sherm Russo in English class. "Or were you just messing with me?"

Sherm got pink—his neck again, Bridge noticed.

"I think it's a possibility," he said. "Anyway, I didn't say it was definitely faked. I said it *looked* fake, those pictures."

"Fake how?"

"You know the one with the astronauts standing next to the American flag?"

"Yeah. I think."

"The flag is waving in the wind, right? It's all rippled, kind of?"

"I guess."

"Well, guess what? There's no wind on the moon."

"There isn't?"

"So the flag should be hanging straight down, like a rag on a pole."

"Huh," Bridge said.

"Exactly. *Huh.*"

"Why would anyone do that? Fake it?"

He laughed. "Ever hear of Sputnik?"

"No," she said.

Their English teacher, who had been reading aloud from a textbook, interrupted himself to say that he had the attention of 70 percent of the class, and that 70 percent was a "dismal figure."

"Anyway," Sherm said quietly, "people fake stuff all the time."

Bridge's homeroom played dodgeball during gym class, the girls against the boys. This time, the girls took their shoes off and were out for blood.

SPUTNIK

"I'm not saying they *couldn't* have faked it," Bridge's mom said that night, passing the taco shells. "I'm saying I don't *believe* they faked it."

"But it's possible."

"Possible? Sure. I mean, today it would be easy, with digital effects, but back then, in the sixties! It would have been staging."

"Staging?" Bridge passed the black beans to her father, who passed them directly to Jamie. Their father didn't "believe in" beans in tacos.

"Like for a play, or a movie—they would have gotten a bunch of rocks and sand to make a fake-moon floor, set up some lights, dressed up in the suits, and taken pictures. Like a photo shoot."

Bridge thought. "And they might have had a giant fan, right? Because in the pictures it looks like the flag is waving, but there's no wind on the moon."

"Really?" Her mom nodded. "Sure, they could have had a fan."

"Or *maybe*," Jamie said, "they dragged a fan *to* the moon. Ever think of *that*?"

"That's dumb," Bridge said.

"Not as dumb as what you're talking about," he said. "Seriously? The moon landings were all faked? Someone should take away your Internet."

"It's not from the Internet. What's Sputnik?"

"Sputnik," their father said, "was the Russians—the Soviet Union, back then. They put the first satellite into orbit, in the 1950s. A very big deal, at the time. The Americans had never done that. It was kind of a challenge—you know, to our national pride."

"So Sputnik was the satellite?"

He nodded. "It was up there for a few months, I think. People here could actually see it in the sky, with the naked eye. And a lot of them didn't like it one bit. That's why Americans were so desperate to get to the moon before the Russians. They called it the Space Race."

"Who wants to go for ice cream?" Bridge's mom said. "We're celebrating. I got a big job today."

Their dad smiled. "A fancy wedding. A *celebrity* wedding."

"Aren, don't be silly—they're only famous for being rich."

"Bo-ring," Jamie said.

"Boring but lucrative," their mom said.

"I want ice cream," Bridge said. "I definitely want ice cream."

Jamie looked at his pedometer. "I have enough juice, I think."

"Juice" meant steps. Jamie was always saying "I'm almost out of juice" or "I need to burn up some of this juice." So far both he and Alex had hit the number ten thousand every single day.

• • •

On the way home from the ice cream place, Jamie, with his chocolate–peanut butter twist, and Bridge, with her banana caramel, walked a few steps behind their parents.

"Are you guys having these intruder drills at your school?" Bridge said.

"Intruder drills?"

"Yeah. I think it's like what to do if a lunatic breaks in? I don't know. We're doing the first one next week."

"Never heard of it. Sounds freaky."

When Bridge didn't respond, he looked at her. "Are you freaked?"

"No." Bridge shrugged.

"Good." Jamie went back to work on his ice cream cone.

"You still haven't told me what you bet Alex," Bridge said.

He shook his head. "I told you, I'm not losing this time. So it's irrelevant."

They stopped short at a corner just as a truck sped through the intersection in front of them. There was a loud bang, like a gun going off, and Bridge's body locked itself down. She couldn't move.

Jamie looked at her. "That was a bottle," he said. "The truck hit a bottle and smashed it." He pointed to a large, curved shard of glass rocking in the middle of the street. "See it?"

"Yeah." Bridge looked at the broken bottle. "I see it." Their light was green, but she couldn't move yet. She saw their parents waiting on the other side of the street, trying to look casual.

Jamie waited while Bridge mentally unlocked her muscles, one at a time.

She took a step. "Yep. All good."

She saw him give their parents a quick thumbs-up, and then he checked his pedometer. "Oops, running on empty." He began taking enormous steps, trying to cover as much ground as he could with each one.

They passed a family whose kids turned, giggling, to watch Jamie lunge down the street.

"Sorry," Jamie said to Bridge. "Is this horribly embarrassing?"

Bridge licked her ice cream and smiled. "Well, yeah," she said. "But only for you."

"Maybe they're staring at your cat ears," Jamie said, lunging again.

"Possible," Bridge said. "But I'm pretty sure they were laughing at you."

Then Jamie grinned. Bridge knew this particular grin. It was his Hermey-the-elf grin.

"Oh no," she said.

"'I don't need anybody,'" Jamie said. "'I'm *independent!*'" It was a line from *Rudolph the Red-Nosed Reindeer*, the Christmas special. They both knew the whole thing by heart because when they were little they liked to act out scenes for their parents. Jamie was always Hermey, the elf who wants to be a dentist, and Bridge was always Rudolph.

She picked up the scene where he had left off: "'Yeah? Me too. I'm . . . whatever you said. *Independent.*'"

"'Hey, what do you say we both be independent together, huh?'"

50

"'You wouldn't mind my red nose?'" Bridge asked.

"'Not if you don't mind me being a dentist,'" Jamie said, lunging again.

Bridge ran to catch up with him, then stuck out her hand to shake. "'It's a deal.'"

THE NINE THOUSAND THINGS

"Aw!" Bridge said, handing the poem back to Emily. "It's sweet." They were standing at their lockers before fourth period.

Emily had written about her little brother, Evan, who was into fortune-telling and robots. The last line was about how he always slept in the bottom bunk of her bed when he had bad dreams, and reading it made Bridge remember that she'd had a nightmare the night before, the usual one, where she was wrapped up tight like a mummy. By the time she'd fought her way out of it, kicking the sheet and blanket off her bed, her mother was next to her, touching her forehead and reminding her to replace the scary picture in her mind the way they'd practiced, with an image of a cold blue sky and clouds moving across it.

Em gazed fondly at her paper. "Yeah, I wrote it this morning in math. When you're weak on effort, it helps to be big on heart."

"That is so cynical!" Tab said.

"Does he really come to your room when he has a nightmare?" Bridge asked.

"Only since the divorce."

Em's parents were the kind who wanted to talk about everything. Her mom wanted to know what Em's friends were "into." She did mother-daughter manicures on Saturdays, and noticed a girl on the train with a thin braid pulled to one side and then practiced so she could do it for Emily. And Em's dad reminded Bridge of Em's mom—he watched reality TV and always knew what meme was going around. They were more alike than any other parents Bridge knew. So it was weird that they were the ones who got divorced.

"Let's say everyone has nine thousand things about themselves," Em had explained to Tab and Bridge in sixth grade, "and say two people fall in love because it *seems* like all their things match up. But what they don't know is that only like a thousand of their things actually match up. My mom says most people who get married don't even *know* those other eight thousand things about themselves yet. So it could happen to anyone."

Now Em belonged to the school's Banana Splits Book Club, for kids whose parents had split up. They read books about other kids whose parents had split up, and talked about them. When Bridge asked her about it, Em just shrugged and said, "Hey, it's free cookies. Mr. P gets black-and-whites from Nussbaum's."

That meant she didn't want to talk about it. But she did say that after her dad moved out, her parents started getting along much better. They even had dinner together once a month.

"You guys." Em slammed her locker. "I'm calling an emergency meeting. Today. At lunch. I need you."

"I can't," Tab said. "I have Hindi Club at lunch on Wednesdays, remember?"

"Bridge?" Em put her hands together under her chin. "Please?"

"I'm supposed to be at that Tech Crew meeting," Bridge said.

"Just tell us now, Em!" Tab said. "Quick! Before the bell rings."

"I can't tell you—I have to *show* you."

"Recess?" Bridge said.

Em shook her head. "It's on my phone. They love snatching phones in the yard. Julie Hopper lost hers on Monday. For two weeks!"

"After last period, then." Tab started walking backward. "Okay?"

TECH CREW

"Okay, people, let's gather stage right. Stage right is on your right if you're standing on the stage facing the audience. *Facing* the audience! Good, here we all are. What nice shiny faces. Hungry? Have some more pizza. This is not school-budget pizza. Budget pizza is only for show nights. I bought this pizza, and I'm not rich, so after today our lunch meetings are brown bag all the way. Got it? Good. C'mon, use the paper plates and the napkins, guys, that's what they're there for.

"Now, there are sixteen of us, and we'll usually meet in two separate groups of eight, a Monday group and a Wednesday group, and then every once in a while we'll all come together, like today.

"First thing I want you to do is form a line—great, nice line, I can tell you guys are pros. Now, one at a time, you're going to strut out onto center stage—yes, *strut*—and face the audience. I know there's nobody out there—just pretend. This is the world of pretend. We are artists and we are servants of the stage, and I take both jobs very seriously. As artists, we work as a collective—all for one and one for all. As servants, we work for those who venture out alone, otherwise known as the performers.

"I want you to know what it feels like to be standing on-stage in front of five hundred and fifty people with those lights shining in your eyes. It's scary, people. And if your microphone cuts out or you trip on a cord in front of those five hundred and fifty people, that's *more* scary. By the way, I say five hundred and fifty people because that's full capacity in this theater—I do not want to hear it referred to as an auditorium! And we always sell out our shows. All five hundred and fifty seats. Always.

"Strut, stand, and imagine. No, don't look away, don't look down, look out *there*. Yes, just like that. What did you say your name was?"

"Sherm."

"No squinting, Sherm. Let those lights smack you right in the eyes. I want you to feel vulnerable. Do you feel vulnerable? Nod once if you feel vulnerable. Good. Do you know why the actors can let themselves feel vulnerable in this theater? Because of us. They may feel alone, but they are not alone. Because we are here, taking care of them. Got it? Good. Who's next?

"Another thing! Everyone wants to know about the black T-shirts. Yes, the shirts are cool. But the shirts, much like today's pizza, are not in the budget. So if you want one, and I hope you do, you have to bring in eight bucks. Shoot, was that the bell already? Last thing! Everyone be quiet. Okay, I'll wait. Good. Listen up. This theater is our sacred space. I said *sacred*. That means whatever may be going on *out there*—in the classrooms, in the yard, in the hallways—means nothing to us in here. Here, we have each other's backs, no matter what. Got it? Everybody nod once if you got it. Good. Class dismissed. Toss your plates in the garbage on your way out."

"Wow," Bridge said, walking next to Sherm as the group filed out of the auditorium. "That kid was right—Mr. Partridge is kind of intense."

"Yeah," Sherm said, blinking double-time. "And I think I'm blind now."

At recess, Sherm ran into the middle of Bridge's kickball game, looking high over his shoulder for a flying football. He missed, ran after it, and picked it up.

"Hey," Bridge called from the outfield. "Do you mind? We're playing a game here!"

"Sorry!" The whole kickball game watched Sherm jog back to the other side of the yard with the football pressed against his stomach. Turning at the last second, he yelled, "I feel so vulnerable right now!" And Bridge laughed.

Em stared after him. "What was that?"

"Inside joke," Bridge said.

The weird thing was that Sherm's flag-on-the-moon theory was all over the Internet: Bridge had looked it up. Lots of people had already talked about it. And it turned out that the astronauts packed a special flag on Apollo 11, with a wire worked into the material so that it would stick out like that. They knew it would just hang down otherwise.

Of course they knew.

VALENTINE'S DAY

The cat has gone to sleep.

You think about curling up next to her and letting the day slip away on fast-forward. But you can't stay here anymore. Your mom might be springing for a cab at this very moment. That thought gets you moving.

You move the plastic dry-cleaning wall to one side, crawl toward the closet door, and listen for footsteps. The apartment is quiet. The neighbor is gone.

Quickly, quickly: you go to your room and grab a five-dollar bill, the only cash you have at the moment, from your desk drawer. Where's your phone? Your idiot neighbor has taken your phone! Unless she just put it down somewhere? You start scanning for it, walking room to room: kitchen, living room—

That's when you hear the toilet flush in the hall bathroom. You freeze. She's still here! You hear water running in the sink. Taking huge steps that are as quiet as you can make them, you cross to the front door, bend down, and pick up your shoes. Then, holding the doorknob so that there is no telltale click, you slip out and close the door behind you.

You sprint down all twelve flights of stairs, hugging the

banister on the turns to make them tight. You're moving so quickly that your momentum pulls you faster and faster, like something getting sucked down a drain.

In the lobby you try to walk casually, as if your scalp isn't pinging with dizziness and fear. You scan the street: there are no cabs pulling up and disgorging screaming mothers. The sidewalk is empty.

INNY

The first intruder drill was scheduled for fifth period, and everyone was even noisier than usual walking into English.

"We don't have closets in this classroom," Bridge's teacher said, after clapping his hands for attention. "So when the drill starts, we'll line up, walk to the back of the room, and crouch against the wall. Any questions?"

Everyone in the class had the same questions: *Closets? Crouch against the wall?* But nobody asked them.

The room was silent. Bridge looked at Sherm, and he looked back. She realized that Sherm's eyes were the same green-gold mix as the eyes of Tab's cat, Sashi.

"What's wrong?" Sherm whispered.

"Nothing," Bridge said.

They listened to the drill announcement on the PA, and when it was over, there was a sound like a loud droning dial tone that made Bridge aware of every other person in the room, as if her body had involuntarily flung little Spider-Man threads to each one of them.

The teacher took a set of keys from his desk drawer and calmly locked the classroom door. He unrolled a little black rectangle of cloth and somehow attached it to the door so that it covered the small window. Bridge wondered what held it there: Double-sided tape? Velcro? Then he switched off the lights.

Their classroom was in the basement, but there was enough light to see by, coming in through a few small windows near the ceiling.

"Quickly and quietly," the teacher said. "Everyone to the back of the room. Don't push your chairs in—leave them." And these were the strangest moments, for Bridge, everyone standing up and walking away from their desks without the usual screech of a hundred chair legs against the floor. She stayed close to Sherm, following the pattern of his plaid shirt in the dim light. They squeezed into the line of kids that stretched across the back of the room.

"Get lower," the teacher said in a quiet voice. "Make your bodies small." Bridge tucked her head down. She could hear Sherm's breathing next to her and smell the smell of his shirt. It smelled like—bread, maybe? Or pancakes?

Sherm appeared to be concentrating on his knees.

Someone started doing the shark music from *Jaws*. There was some nervous giggling. But mostly they were quiet. She knew it was only a drill, but it got a little creepy, with everyone hunched in the dark. Bridge kept her eyes on the door. Her folded legs began to ache. Every once in a while, she glanced at Sherm, being careful to keep her body still, to move only her eyes. But he seemed to feel her looking, and always raised his head a little to look back at her.

Then Sherm whispered. "Hey. What'd you have for breakfast this morning?"

She whispered back. "Breakfast?"

"Yeah. I had an egg sandwich. What'd you have?"

"Oh—cereal. And cinnamon toast."

"I've never tried cinnamon toast."

"Are you serious?"

He locked eyes with her. "I wouldn't lie about a thing like that."

"Do you know where they have the best cinnamon toast?" Bridge whispered. "At the Dollar-Eight Diner."

"Yeah?" Sherm hesitated. "Want to go? To Dollar-Eight?"

"When?"

"What about next Friday? After school?"

Bridge nodded. "I think we have to. I mean, you can't say 'cinnamon toast' and not want cinnamon toast. It's like an automatic response, right?"

He smiled. "Sure."

The PA speaker came back to life with a loud static pop that made everyone jump.

"He likes you, you know," Em said after school. "That kid Sherm."

"Don't be nuts."

"I'm not being nuts."

They'd gathered outside for Em's "emergency meeting." Bridge was still in a bad mood from French, where all the words bounced off her, where she waited with a growing sense of doom for Madame Lawrence to point with that look on her face, like she was waiting for Bridge to stop being so stubborn and speak French already.

"So? The suspense is killing me!" Tab said to Emily. "What are you showing us?"

"This." Em held out her phone. "Look at *this*."

Tab and Bridge leaned over it.

It was a picture of a—

"What the heck is *that*?" Tab snatched the phone and held it close to her face.

"Do you need glasses?" Em said. "It's a belly button."

"That is NOT your belly button," Tab said. "No offense, but we all know you have an outie."

Emily grabbed for her phone, but Tab held on to it. "Let *Bridge* see it!" Em said. "And of course it isn't my belly button. Would I call an emergency meeting to show you a picture of my belly button?" She got the phone from Tab and handed it to Bridge. "And just for the record, Tab, I happen to like my belly button. It's awesome. You idiot."

"So—this is Patrick's belly button?" Bridge asked.

"Shhh! *Yes!*" Em shrieked. Then in a lower voice, "It's Patrick's."

Tab made a face. "Ugh. I really wish you hadn't shown me that. Celeste is waiting for me. I have to go to the stupid orthodontist."

"Wait!" Em said. "You guys haven't helped me at *all*."

"Helped with what?"

"With the whole *picture* thing."

"You want help erasing that ugly picture?" Tab said. "Why didn't you say so?"

HOW TO MAKE A FIST

On her way home from school, Bridge stopped at the Bean Bar. Adrienne was behind the doughnut counter, wearing a T-shirt that said THROW LIKE A GIRL.

"Is my dad around?" Bridge asked.

"He's at an event." Adrienne started jumping from side to side, fast little hops with her feet together. "One of those office-party gigs."

"Oh." Bridge watched Adrienne jump. Her blond hair was in a lot of messy braids that bounced, but the rest of her was small and compact. She had what Bridge's mom called a heart-shaped face, and a chin with a tiny dimple in it.

"Have a seat," Adrienne said, gesturing at the mostly empty tables.

Bridge sat.

"You want a doughnut, Finnegan?"

Bridge glanced around. "Um, my name's Bridge."

Still jumping, Adrienne nodded. "I knew a kid named Finnegan who always sat like that, on the edge of his chair, with his backpack on and everything. Like he was ready to bolt. Sometimes he'd be sitting on our couch in a winter coat all afternoon, playing video games." She laughed. "So do you want a doughnut?" Bouncing, she pointed one hand like a gun at the doughnut tray.

"Nah."

"Cookie? Muffin?"

"No thanks." Bridge had never turned down a cookie from Mark, but Adrienne made her nervous.

"I have a brother too," Adrienne said.

"What?"

"Like you. A brother. In Canada. Finnegan was his friend, actually. Not mine."

"You grew up in Canada?"

Still jumping, Adrienne nodded and pointed at herself with both thumbs. "French Canadian." She smiled.

"You speak French?"

"In school it was mostly English. But my dad was always making me speak French at home. I hated it."

"You're lucky, though. I mean, now you speak two languages, right?"

"Yeah. Three, if you count body language." She laughed, moved her hands to her hips, and started jumping an invisible jump rope.

"Is that, like, exercise?"

"I like to move around. That's why I'm a pretty decent boxer."

Bridge laughed.

"What's funny, Finnegan? I box. This place is more like a day job. You know what a day job is?"

"A job you do during the day?"

"No. A day job is a meaningless job that pays. No offense to your dad."

Bridge didn't know what to say to that. "I'm terrible at languages," she blurted. "The worst."

Adrienne smiled, still jumping. "But do you know how to throw a punch?"

"What?"

"A punch." Adrienne punched the air, two quick jabs.

"I guess so." Bridge's hands clenched at her sides.

"You a righty?"

"Yeah."

"Make a fist. Can't throw a punch if you don't know how to make a fist."

Bridge made a fist and raised it in front of her. It made her think about that year of rehab after the accident: "Pick up the pen. Put it down. Walk to the door. Now come back." She looked at her fist. She was still surprised by the lack of pain sometimes.

"What's that?" Adrienne said. "That's your fist?" She stopped jumping. "Come here."

Bridge went up to the counter, and Adrienne came out from behind it to stand in front of her. "A good fist has no air in it," Adrienne told her. "First, fold your fingers down, tips to base. Yeah. Now fold them again, toward that meat below your thumb. Right. Now tuck your thumb up to hold it all together. *Much* better."

Bridge had never in her life thought about the right way or wrong way to make a fist, but standing there in the Bean Bar, she felt strong. She thought about the nonexistent intruder at school. She smiled and threw an air punch toward Adrienne.

"All wrong," Adrienne said flatly. "Don't square your body like that—put one leg back, and when you throw the punch, your weight should be shifting. Body in motion, body *always* in motion. Your other hand should be up by your face, not hanging dead at your side like that. And you want to lead with your knuckles, not the thumb. If you lead with your thumb, you're going to do damage to no one but yourself. Let's see it again. Yeah, better. There's hope for you."

Bridge dropped her arms. "Thanks."

"You sure you don't want a cookie, Finnegan? Or how about some of this sticky stuff over here?" She pointed.

Bridge smiled. "That's halvah. My dad loves it."

Adrienne looked up. "Armenian thing?"

Bridge laughed. "Yeah. Armenians like it. But so do other people."

"I tried it the other day—it's kind of like fudge without the chocolate."

"It's sesame," Bridge said.

"Sesame! Full of protein." Adrienne reached for the tray. "Come on, one for me and one for you."

SHERM

October 14

Dear Nonno Gio,
   I got a 102 on my math test. Mr. Fisher had me do the extra-credit problem on the board.
   Nonna made the Marsala chicken tonight. Sometimes when she brings the food to the table I know we're all thinking about you but nobody says anything. Dad gets this look on his face. Sometimes I get so mad at you I almost wish you were dead. I don't wish that, though.
   She's still wearing those cat ears.

                                        Sherm

P.S. Four months until your birthday.

DOLLAR-EIGHT

The waitress at the diner seemed genuinely happy to see Bridge. "Hey there, Cinnamon Toast. Little while no see!" She grabbed two menus from a stack and handed them to Sherm, winking at him. "Sit anywhere, guys. I'll be right with you."

Sherm was impressed. "You weren't kidding—she really does call you Cinnamon Toast."

Bridge smiled and slid into a booth. "Are you opposed to splitting a vanilla shake?"

Sherm said he wasn't at all opposed to a vanilla shake.

"Good. Because a vanilla shake goes really well with cinnamon toast."

Sherm grinned.

She kept waiting for the strangeness to arrive—being at the diner with Sherm Russo. This is strange, she told herself. They'd met in front of school and walked here together, pretending it was perfectly normal, which it wasn't. Only it didn't exactly feel strange, either.

Bridge had once read a story about a girl who goes on a date to a restaurant where she's too shy to order anything but the cheapest thing on the menu, which is a cream cheese and olive sandwich.

"Have you ever had a cream cheese and olive sandwich?" she asked Sherm. Not that this was a date.

"No," Sherm said. "Have you?"

"No." They looked at their menus. "You can order anything you want," Bridge said. "I have money."

"Thanks. But we came for cinnamon toast, right?"

The waitress came back with two glasses of water. "You guys know what you want?"

"Two orders of cinnamon toast, please," Bridge said. "And a vanilla shake in two glasses."

The waitress smiled. "You sure you need two glasses? I could bring one glass and two straws." She winked again.

"Two glasses," Bridge said. "Please."

Suddenly she worried that when the waitress walked away and she and Sherm were sitting across the table from each other with no menus between them, they would have nothing to say to each other. There would be what Jamie called awkward silence.

That was what Jamie said whenever the conversation died down at dinner: "Awkward silence." And when their mother said, "It's *comfortable* silence, Jamie. There's nothing awkward about it," Jamie would wait a beat and then say, very doubtfully, "If you say so." Once, this routine had made Emily laugh so hard she practically snorted her dinner through her nose and had to leave the table to pull herself together in the bathroom.

"You know that riddle?" Bridge said to Sherm. "With the two brothers guarding the two doors, and one door leads to heaven and the other one leads to hell?"

Sherm shook his head. "Never heard of it."

"Really?" Bridge leaned forward. "So there are two brothers. One brother always lies, and one brother always tells the truth. You want the door to heaven, obviously, but you're only allowed to ask one question."

"One question each?"

"No. One question."

"Do I know which brother is which?"

Bridge thought. "No. You don't know which is which."

The waitress brought their food, and Sherm picked up two toast halves together, like a sandwich.

"Stop!" Bridge said. "What are you doing?"

Sherm's hand froze. "Eating my cinnamon toast?"

"You can't eat it like that! You have to eat one piece at a time, faceup, so that the cinnamon and the sugar hit the roof of your mouth."

Separating the two sides of his toast, Sherm muttered, "You're lucky I'm used to living with bossy women."

"Very funny." Bridge felt herself go red. "I'm just trying to give you the real experience here."

Sherm took a bite of the cinnamon toast.

"Well?" Bridge said.

"It's delicious," Sherm said. He bowed his head. "Thank you for showing me your planet."

"You're hilarious."

"I especially enjoy the way the cinnamon and sugar feel against the roof of my mouth."

"Double hilarious. Just go ahead and pretend this isn't the best thing ever."

"It is, actually," Sherm said, looking her straight in the eyes, the way he had during the intruder drill. "Best thing ever."

Bridge pushed his glass toward him. "And you haven't even tried it with the shake!"

There were no awkward silences. When the check came, they each paid four dollars. Bridge never left less than a twenty percent tip. Her mom said that was the definition of a good New Yorker.

"Nice wallet," Bridge told Sherm. "Looks about a hundred years old!" She grabbed it. "Check out all the secret pockets!" She turned it upside down, and something fell to the table.

It was a worn square of paper with a date written on it in big letters.

"What's February fourteenth?" Bridge asked, reading upside down. She felt bad all of a sudden, about grabbing the wallet and shaking it like that. She closed it and held it out to Sherm.

He took the wallet and then picked up the slip of paper from the table.

"It's Valentine's Day, dummy."

"And you just like to carry that piece of information around so you don't forget?"

"Actually, this was my grandfather's wallet. And this"—he held up the paper—"is his birthday."

"Oh God, sorry," Bridge said. "I didn't—"

"He's not dead," Sherm said quickly. "He moved out over the summer. My grandparents always lived with us, but now it's just my grandmother. He left her, after fifty years."

"Oh. Wow. Where did he go?"

Sherm made a face. "He moved to New Jersey."

Watching Sherm tuck the slip of paper into his wallet so carefully, Bridge felt even worse. "I'm sorry," she said. "That really sucks."

"I write to him sometimes," Sherm said. "Letters. Do you think that's weird?"

"It's not weird. It's nice. Does he write you back?"

Sherm looked up. "I haven't actually mailed any of them."

"Why not?"

He shrugged. "He doesn't deserve letters. He just left. My dad says he's moving in with some woman he met. Which feels kind of crazy, to tell you the truth, because he's a great person. I mean, he was. We don't really talk about it much. That's another crazy thing, not talking about it. But my parents are really busy and my grandmother only likes to talk about happy things. Happy things, or books."

Bridge nodded. "I get that."

Sherm rubbed the worn leather of the wallet with his thumbs. "I remember when you got hit by that car," he said.

There was a funny feeling that traveled down Bridge's legs sometimes—a zinging rush to her feet. "You do?"

"Yeah. It was right at the end of my block."

"Your block? That's so random. I didn't realize you even knew about that." She laughed. "Even I forget about it sometimes."

"Everybody knows about it." Sherm raised his head and the light hit his eyes. Now they looked greenish-blue mixed with light brown. Bridge thought they looked like tiny planet Earths. "What was it like?" he asked.

"The accident? I don't remember it. All I remember is the

75

hospital—the nurses, and stupid stuff like these paper menus they had with pictures of animals all over them that you were supposed to color in with these broken crayons. I remember that."

"You almost died, my dad said."

"Yeah, everyone says that. But I don't remember it."

Now Sherm stacked sugar packets on the tabletop, carefully shaking each one first to make it lie flat. "My grandparents went to the hospital," he said. "That first night. They sat in the lobby."

"Really?" That was strange to think about.

Sherm looked at her. "A bunch of people were there, my dad said."

"Who?"

"Just people. From the neighborhood, I guess. The next day my grandmother wanted me to pray with her, but I ran out of her room." His eyes flicked to Bridge's, then back to his sugar tower. "I feel weirdly bad about that."

"That's okay." Bridge got an achy feeling at the bottom of her throat and took a sip of her water. "You were just a little kid. It wouldn't have made a difference. I mean, I'm fine!" She reached her arms up over her head and wiggled her fingers as if this were universal proof of being fine.

Sherm smiled. "Yeah."

"Actually," she said, "I lied before. I don't ever forget about the accident."

He nodded, unsurprised.

Bridge hesitated. "After the accident, this nurse at the hospital told me that I'm here for a reason."

"Here?"

Bridge nodded. "She said that's why I didn't die. It kind of weirds me out, actually."

He was the first person she'd ever told. She hadn't planned to tell him—she hardly knew him. It had something to do with how he had tucked that little piece of paper back into that cruddy wallet. The way he seemed to meet her thoughts wherever they went. The look on his face.

Sherm said, "My grandfather used to say that everyone alive has already beaten the craziest odds, just being born. Like one in a trillion. Your parents could have had a million different kids, but they had you. And before that could happen, your parents had to be born themselves, and *their* parents had to be born." He picked up his shake and used the straw to vacuum the bottom of the glass. "I mean, think about it. It goes all the way back."

Bridge laughed. "I don't know if that makes me feel better or worse."

"Maybe it should just make you feel lucky. Yeah, you were really lucky you didn't die after the accident. But you were a lot luckier to be born in the first place. So if you're here for a reason, maybe we all are."

"I guess. Yeah."

"You never told me the answer to that riddle."

"Oh," Bridge said. Then she laughed again. "You know what? I can't remember."

SHERM

October 24

Dear Nonno Gio,

   Nonna made lasagna and you're pretty sad you missed it, even if you don't know it.

   I tried cinnamon toast today and it was great. Do you think people are born for a special purpose? I don't. I think it's just something that happens.

Sherm

P.S. Three months, twenty-one days until your birthday.

VALENTINE'S DAY

You have to tell your mom you aren't in a ditch. That's kind of weighing on you. There's a copy shop on Broadway, near the university, where you think you can get online. You'll send her an email.

You turn north, pull your hood up again, and play hot lava all the way there.

The copy place is busy: there are college kids sitting at computer terminals, two men with a stroller at the counter, and people waiting for the copiers. You get in line behind the couple with the baby and watch a woman struggle with a color copier. She keeps hitting the big green button, but nothing is happening. A man in a down jacket is using the paper cutter near the door, trimming a stack of pale blue cards. Invitations, you think. He pauses. Walks over to the woman at the copier. "Not working?" he says.

She gives him a frustrated smile.

After the apocalypse, they'll have three kids, you decide. The middle kid will turn out to be some kind of genius. The younger one will be an artist. The older one might marry the baby in the stroller, who's trying to jam his straw into his juice box. He's having problems. Don't worry, you think at him. After the apocalypse, there will be no more juice boxes.

Gina invented the apocalypse game. The game sounds creepy but it isn't. Not super-creepy, anyway.

"What if there was a nuclear bomb, and only the people in this room survived?" Gina asked one day last fall. You remember that she was wearing a sweatshirt with a picture of Smurfette on it. You were at Dollar-Eight, feeling relaxed and goofy. No Vinny.

"Nuclear bomb, nice thought," you said.

"Yeah, but who do you think you'd end up with? I mean, we'd all have to pair up and have babies, right? To repopulate the planet." Gina scanned the diner. "Oh, I think I want him."

From her lap, she mini-pointed to a kid sitting alone near the window, reading a paperback.

You'd laughed. "So everyone we know is dead and your first thought is dating?"

Gina looked fake-hurt. "For the sake of the human race."

"Okay. I'll take the one at the counter. We both like French fries."

She leaned, looked. "I approve. So what about everyone else?"

And the two of you sat, arranging families and assigning jobs.

"Those two are made for each other!"

"He looks like a doctor, doesn't he?"

"That woman is definitely the president of something—look at those killer shoes. She can be in charge."

"Okay. But she still needs a love life. . . ."

That was the game.

"We'll stay best friends, of course," Gina said that day. "Those girls in that booth over there look nice too. They can hang with us."

Best friends. You remember the happiness of that.

At the copy shop, you play the game by yourself, feeling in your pocket again and again for your phone. It's beyond weird to be without it.

Every time the door swings open, your fragile world gets a little more broken. First, the color-copier lady leaves without even saying goodbye to the blue-invitations man, and their three kids evaporate like mist. Then the woman in the funky glasses walks away from her true love in the suede shirt at computer terminal #3. He doesn't care, just stares at the document on his screen as if nothing has happened. It's sad. Everything they would have come to feel for each other— gone.

You reach *again* for your phone without meaning to. Stupid neighbor.

OR IS SHE A WOMAN?

Bridge loved Tab's living room: the plants on the window-sills, the black-and-white photographs on the walls, the jars of nail polish scattered across the coffee table like pretty rocks. There were sheer ivory curtains under embroidered turquoise ones and small brass sculptures on the bookshelves. Bridge couldn't remember if they were from France, where Tab's parents lived before they had kids, or from India, where they were born. She loved the way her feet sank into the carpet, the bowls of salty soy nuts, the way their cat snuggled with them on the couch. Jamie was allergic to cats.

"What do you think goes through her mind when she looks in the mirror?" Bridge said. She and Tab were on a homework break, huddled in front of a laptop on the couch, looking at a picture of Julie Hopper, the eighth grader from Em's soccer team who'd had her legs across Em's lap during the clubs fair. "Does she see what we see? Like how other people see her? I mean, *boom*, she's beautiful. You know?"

"Well, *I* see her as kind of naked," Tab said, clicking the picture to make it bigger. "Like a naked person with a towel over her shoulders."

"She's wearing a bathing suit. Everyone looks half naked in a bathing suit."

Celeste, Tab's sister, walked in and said, "Who's naked? That's *my* laptop, Tab, bought with *my* babysitting money. You're supposed to ask first, remember?" She dropped down on the couch next to them. "Hold the phone. That's Julie Hopper? When did she get so gorgeous? Wait—she put that up on her own page? It kind of looks like she's not wearing pants."

"It's a bathing suit," Bridge said.

"Oh. Maybe the angle is weird. Looks like she forgot to put on pants."

"See?" Tab said. "Told you."

"You know Julie Hopper?" Bridge asked Celeste.

Celeste looked at her. "I actually went to your middle school, remember? Last year? I was the one with the gorgeous bod and the perfect makeup?"

Bridge smiled. "I remember. I just didn't know you knew Julie."

"She's only a year behind me. Last spring, some poor kid wrote her a letter about how much he liked her and she read it to her homeroom. She was famous for at least a week after that."

"Wow—that's mean," Bridge said.

"He probably deserved it," Tab said.

"Eighty-eight comments!" Celeste said, squinting at the screen. "Bridge, scroll down."

Bridge scrolled down, reading the comments on Julie's page, mostly things like "Gorgeous!" and "So hot!"

Em had written: OMG. *I wish I was you. Serious.*

And Julie had written back: *Aw thanks! ILY.*

And Em had written back: *ILYSM.*

"Don't worry," Celeste said, looking at Tab and Bridge. "You guys just haven't, you know, grown those parts yet. Julie's a year older than you are. You'll look just like that! More or less."

"Do I look worried? I'm not worried," Tab said.

Tab would probably look like Celeste, Bridge thought. Celeste had the kind of body Bridge would want, if she could choose: not too much, not too little.

"I'm just saying it seems like a big deal, but it isn't." Celeste threw her shoulders back and took a deep breath, which pushed her chest out and made Bridge think that Celeste actually did think it was kind of a big deal.

"Again," Tab said, "not worried."

"Do you guys ever watch *The Twilight Zone?*" Bridge asked.

"The vampire books?" Celeste asked vaguely. She had taken control of the laptop and was scrolling through Julie Hopper's photos.

"No, *The Twilight Zone*. It was this old show on TV. These different stories."

"Sounds cute."

"They're kind of creepy, actually. There's this one about a woman in a hospital bed and her whole head is wrapped up in gauze. Just her head. And the nurses—but you can only see their hands, not their faces—are starting to unwrap her. And the doctor, but you can't see him either, you can only hear his voice, is telling her she shouldn't get her hopes up, because the surgery might not have been successful."

"Notice how the nurses are women and the doctor is a man?" Tab said, nodding.

"I didn't say the nurses were women," Bridge said.

"Oh. Were they?"

"Yes," Bridge admitted.

"Ha!" Tab said.

"Shush. So finally the bandages fall away and she's *perfect*. She's, like, ridiculously beautiful. The room goes silent, someone passes her a mirror, and then she starts screaming her head off. She's *horrified* by what she sees in the mirror."

"I don't get it," Tab said.

"You're not supposed to yet. *Then* the camera pulls back and for the first time you see the faces of the doctors and nurses in the room, and they all look like *pigs*! They have these *snouts*!"

"What?" Celeste looked up, suddenly interested.

"Snouts! Like *pigs*! It's this other reality, where she looks like a supermodel but *she's* the ugly one. Get it?"

"I wouldn't want to live on a planet where everyone looks like a pig." Celeste fake-shuddered.

"You're missing the point," Bridge said.

"Maybe you had to be there." Celeste closed her laptop and looked at Bridge. "Your hair is getting so long. Have you ever tried a messy bun?"

"Messy bun?" Tab said. "Is that to eat? Mmm, messy bun. Sounds delicious."

"Don't be mental."

"Mental," Tab told Bridge, as if Celeste weren't sitting right there. "She gets that from these hair videos she watches on YouTube. A lot of the girls are British. Now she runs around saying everything is either 'brilliant' or 'mental.'"

"I do not. But, Bridge, did you know there are like a hundred thousand videos on the Internet about how to put your hair up or do your makeup? It's this whole *world* of information."

"Yeah, I'm pretty sure that's why they invented the Internet," Tab said.

"You know what, Tab? You don't have to make a statement every five seconds." Celeste looked at Bridge thoughtfully. "Or maybe a sock bun."

"What's a sock bun?" Bridge asked.

"Mmm, sock bun," Tab said. "Sounds delicious."

"It's a bun rolled up around a sock," Celeste told Bridge. "Looks prettier than it sounds. And your hair is so dark and heavy . . . it'll be beautiful. Even with the cat ears." She paused, leaned back. "You know, I think I like the ears. They give you some nice height."

Tab burst out laughing. "Tell me you didn't just say that."

"Ignore her," Celeste instructed Bridge. "Want to try it? The sock bun?"

"Uh. Maybe," Bridge said.

"I'll go get the stuff!" Celeste jumped up, glanced at herself in the mirror hanging over the couch, and did a double take.

"No. No! It's still there. It's—*bigger!*"

"What is?" Bridge asked.

"She can't pass a mirror without looking at herself," Tab said.

"This zit!" Celeste turned, her finger aimed at a place to the left of her chin. "I paid, like, twenty-eight dollars for this stupid cream that was supposed to boost my radiance. What did I get for it? A four-dimensional zit!"

"It's tiny," Bridge said. "I didn't even see it until you pointed."

Tab rolled her eyes. "Four dimensions? Does it smell or something?"

"Ew, no. The fourth dimension is *time*. This thing has been here for two weeks!"

Tab said, "Stop laughing, Bridge. You're encouraging her."

Celeste glared at the spot in the mirror. "Leave, thing! *Leave!*"

"I can't help it," Bridge said. "She's funny!"

"You realize our fifteen-minute break was over half an hour ago, right?" Tab pointed to their books on the coffee table.

Celeste spun away from the mirror and squinted at the computer. "Is it four-thirty? I'm so sorry, Bridge, I have to pick up Evan from computer club. I'll show you the sock bun later, okay? Promise."

"Anyway, we're supposed to be doing French," Tab told Bridge. "Remember? Did you look at the flash cards I made you?"

"Sort of." Bridge rooted around in her backpack for her flash cards. "There's this new girl at the Bean Bar. She says French is the language of love. And that's why she refuses to speak it."

Tab made a face. "That's stupid. How can there be a language of love? And Bridge, is she really a 'girl'? Or is she a woman?"

AWKWARD SILENCE

Bridge looked at herself in the mirror on the back of her bedroom door. Really *looked*.

Then she put on her cat ears, felt them settle like a hand on her head.

"*Il pleut,*" she told herself. *It's raining.*

French even made her mouth look stupid.

She had dressed carefully, in dark jeans and the black Charlie Chaplin T-shirt her mom had given her for her birthday.

In the kitchen she found Jamie on his knees, trying to reach a box of cereal on the counter. "Can you push it toward me a little?" he asked.

Bridge moved the box to the edge of the counter. Jamie grabbed it, tucked it under one arm, and crawled to the refrigerator, where he took out the milk.

"You can't be out of steps already," Bridge said. "It's seven-twenty-five in the morning."

"Track practice today. I have to save up. Can you grab me a bowl?"

Bridge was early to school, where kids were lined up against the fence in a chilly wind, waiting for the main doors to open. Most of them were looking at their phones for those last few minutes before they had to be powered down until three o'clock.

Bridge walked to the end of the line, realizing as she got closer that Sherm was standing there with his phone, scrolling with a thumb. A quick electric shower broke over her.

"Hey," she said.

Sherm looked up and smiled. "Oh, hey."

She dropped her book bag between her feet. *Please, no awkward silence.*

"Hey," Sherm said again, this time to someone behind her. Bridge turned to look.

"Dude," a tall kid said to Sherm. They bumped elbows.

"This is Patrick," Sherm said. "He's in eighth."

"Yeah, but this genius is in my math class," Patrick said.

Emily's Patrick, Bridge realized. He had longish brown hair and big brown eyes and wore a navy-blue hoodie. He looked cold. I've seen your belly button! she thought. Her eyes drifted down his hoodie, but she caught herself and brought them up again.

A whistle blew, the school doors opened, and the line started to shuffle forward. Bridge wanted Patrick to say something else—something she could bring back for Emily.

"I'm Bridge," she said. Because Sherm hadn't said her name.

"I know. Em's friend. The cat girl." He nodded at her ears.

"Yeah." She smiled.

"Houdini, right?" He pointed at her T-shirt.

Bridge glanced down. "Actually, it's Charlie Chaplin."

"Right! That's what I meant."

She couldn't think of anything else to say. She couldn't seem to think of anything but his belly button.

SHERM

Sherm's grandfather was the one who'd hooked Sherm on math.

"Hey. How long until my birthday?" he asked five-year-old Sherm one afternoon in the park. They'd been collecting leaves from the cobblestones: red, orange, yellow, green. Each of them had a fistful.

"Your birthday?" asked Sherm, who had only given any serious thought to his own birthday.

"Yes, my birthday." His grandfather poked himself in the chest with two fingers. "Old people have birthdays too, you know. And I like to have something to look forward to. So—how long do I have to wait?"

Sherm had no idea.

"Tell you what," his grandfather said. "I'm going to write down my birthday on a piece of paper, and I'm going to give that paper to you. And from now on, you're my man. Whenever I want to know how long until my birthday, I'm coming to you. Do we have a deal?"

And then his grandfather had explained how to count forward by months and days. There was some tricky stuff: he'd told Sherm about short months and long months, and showed him how to count on his knuckles to figure out which months were which.

"How long?" he'd ask Sherm as they were putting on their boots or loading the dishwasher or waiting to check out books at the library. And Sherm would do the calculation in his head. He'd liked math ever since.

VALENTINE'S DAY

"Can I help you?" The guy behind the counter at the copy shop is cute, with spiky hair. *Too cool for school*, Gina would say.

"Yeah," you tell him. "I need, like, one minute online."

"Four ninety-five," he says. He glances over your head at the computer stations. "You can have terminal one."

"Five dollars? For one minute?"

Five dollars is all you have. You planned to get a bagel or something.

He looks at you. "Yeah. It's four ninety-five for the first five minutes."

"I only need *one* minute."

He smiles and gets even cuter. "Sorry. It doesn't work that way. If my boss weren't here, I'd let you hop on, but—" His hand knocks the counter, twice. "You know how it is."

"Yeah, I totally get it." You hand over your five-dollar bill.

He punches the register open. "Drop/add?"

"What?"

"Drop/add. The deadline is noon, right?" He tilts his head at the campus gate across the street. "It's always busy here on drop/add day."

He thinks you're in college. "Oh yeah. Thanks."

"Well, good luck." He hands you a nickel. "Happy Valentine's Day."

"Yeah, you too."

You sit at the computer, open the browser, and log in. There are three emails waiting from your mom, all written in the subject lines.

Where are you?

Call me immediately—I'm worried.

Honey, call my cell. On my way home.

Your mom is great. She's the best. But there's no way you're going to call her. She'll want you to come home right now for a heart-to-heart. She'll want to tell you that none of this is very important.

You write back:

Hi, Mom—I'm ok, just need ONE mental-health day, see you later and pls don't worry at ALL.

And then you hit send, log out, and quit the browser. Just to be thorough.

You glance at the time in the upper right corner of the screen and calculate what you'd be doing at school. It's almost homeroom. Homeroom is when they'll hand out the flowers.

You leave the copy store quickly, as if the police might have traced your email, as if they're throwing themselves into their squad cars and converging on your location.

"Happy Valentine's Day," the spiky-hair guy calls as you leave.

"Yeah, you said that already," you mumble.

Outside, you walk a couple of quick blocks and then stop to look around: people with their coffee cups, people with their phones, people with their friends. It dawns on you again that you're hungry. You feel for your purse, your wallet, your phone. And you remember. You don't have your purse. You don't have your wallet. You don't have your phone. You can't go home right now. And aside from that nickel, you have no money at all.

"Mental-health day." Those are Vinny's words, stuck in your head along with so much else of her, and you wish you hadn't used them.

THREES ARE HARD

"*Halloween*, remember?" Tab said, hands on her hips. "This is a Halloween-*only* meeting!" They were at the minimart after school, in the back.

"Fine." Em jammed her phone into her jeans pocket. She'd been showing them a picture of Patrick's doorknob. The doorknob to his bedroom, he said.

"Bridge! Pay attention!" Tab clapped twice, like a teacher.

"I *am* paying attention," Bridge said, scanning the cookie aisle.

Tab said, "Halloween! Come on, guys. Ideas?"

"Something that comes in threes," Bridge said.

"Like poison ivy?" Tab said. "Leaves of three?"

"No, not like poison ivy," Bridge said.

"I am not being a leaf for Halloween!" Em said.

"Shhh. Think. Things in threes."

"The three bears," Tab said.

"Three billy goats gruff," Bridge said.

"I'm not being a bear or a goat," Em said. "Those sound ugly."

"Well, it's not a sex parade," Tab snapped.

"Shut up, Tab! Who said anything about a sex parade?"

"You know what I mean," Tab said. "I'm not doing one of those stupid girl costumes that society is always trying to force on us, like a nurse in a miniskirt or a maid in fishnet stockings."

"The Berperson is brainwashing you. You realize that, right?" Em put her hands on her hips. "What does she think you should be for Halloween? A Teletubby?"

"Oooh," Tab said. "Look who's coming."

It was Patrick, with a bunch of other eighth graders, including Julie Hopper, who patted Em on the head as she passed. They swarmed into the back of the minimart, opening and slamming fridge doors, grabbing Gatorades and bags of chips.

"Hey, you," Patrick said to Em. He stopped and held up one clenched hand for a fist bump, which Em executed flawlessly.

Tab rolled her eyes.

"Hey," he said to Bridge, smiling.

"Hey," Bridge said. Patrick was only one grade above them, but something about him was older, as if he'd crossed a line Bridge couldn't even see yet.

"Hi, Patrick," Tab said in a cartoon-girl voice, making every syllable twice as long as it should have been. "Nice doorknob."

He pretended not to hear. Julie Hopper yelled from the front of the store, "Patrick! Be my cash machine? I only have two bucks."

"Um, sure!" Patrick followed the rest of his crowd up to the register.

Em turned on Tab. "What did you do that for?"

"Just making conversation. Geez. You're bright red."

"That was seriously stupid, Tab. Now he knows I've been talking about his pictures."

"Sorry! It was a joke!" Tab smiled.

Em stared at her. "How do you not see how rude you just were?"

"I said sorry." Tab shrugged. "I didn't realize he meant that much to you."

"You don't sound sorry."

"Em, I really am sorry. Okay? Anyway, no fighting allowed. Remember?"

Emily zipped her sweatshirt up to her chin. "I have to go to soccer practice. Do we have a decision about Halloween?"

"A decision? We're still brainstorming!" Tab said.

"What about superheroes?" Bridge said.

"Superheroes?" Em looked doubtful.

"Yeah, you know, like Batgirl, Catgirl—"

"Notice how the male superheroes are all 'this-man' and 'that-man'? And the females are all 'girls'? Super*man*, Super-*girl*. Bat*man*, Bat*girl*."

"There's Wonder Woman," Bridge said.

"Okay," Tab said. "I'll be Wonder Woman. She has a cape, right? I love capes!" She started zooming around with her arms stuck out in front of her.

"Okay," Em said. "You're Wonder Woman. Obviously Bridge will be Catgirl. So I'll be Batgirl."

"Why is that obvious?" Bridge asked.

"Are you kidding?" Em pointed at Bridge's head. "It'll be

the one day of the year that those ears aren't completely random."

Tab stopped zooming. "They are just a tiny bit random, Bridge."

"They don't feel random to me."

"What do they feel like to you?" Em asked. "Why are you wearing them? Every. Single. Day."

"Because I want to? They feel like me."

Tab and Emily looked at each other. "They're cat ears," Em said. "Do you feel like a cat?"

"No," Bridge said.

"Guys," Tab said. "Let's put a pin in this." Tab had been saying that lately. As if you could really take a moment, stick a pin in it, and save it for later.

Tab turned to Bridge. "You coming over to do French?"

"Yeah," Bridge said.

"Anyway," Tab said as they walked to the register together, "there are *four* Teletubbies."

MOON HUNTING

"You guys want soup?" Celeste stuck her head into the living room, where Bridge and Tab had done what felt like hours of French.

"Mom called," Celeste said to Tab. "She's on her way home, but remember, dinner's gonna be late."

"Oh yeah," Tab said. "Poor Mom."

"Why?" Bridge said.

"Today is Karva Chauth," Celeste said. "Good Hindu women fast all day to show their devotion to their husbands."

"For real?" Bridge asked.

"For real," Tab said. "It brings luck, they say. They can't eat or drink or anything, not even water, which is a little crazy if you ask me."

"Until they glimpse the moon," Celeste said. "I think it's kind of romantic."

"Romantic to starve yourself all day?" Tab asked. "And is there a day when the husbands fast for their wives? No, of course not!"

"Oy, the big feminist," Celeste said. "It's getting old, Tab. So—two soups?"

"Two soups," Bridge said. "Thanks."

Ten minutes later, Celeste brought out a tray with three bowls of tomato rice soup and a plate of saltines. "There's one Karva Chauth story about this young queen," she said, crossing her legs on the couch. "She fasts to bring her new husband good luck, and by the end of the day she's really thirsty and weak with hunger but the moon isn't up yet, and her seven brothers can't stand to watch her suffer anymore—"

"So they trick her," Tab said.

"I'm telling it, Tab! So they trick her. They put a mirror up in a tree and pretend it's the moon. She sees it shining through the branches. So she eats."

"And then—BOOM—her husband drops dead!" Tab clapped once, on the *boom*.

"I said I'm telling it! He doesn't die, Tab, he gets really sick. And then she feels terrible, she's a mess. She takes care of him for a year and then this god feels sorry for her and makes him better."

"I heard he died," Tab said. "And the queen takes care of his dead body for a year. And that's when the god feels sorry for her. So the god brings him back to life."

"Girls!" Tab's mom stood in the doorway in her socks, holding her briefcase. She looked at Bridge. "That's only one story—there are others. Less gruesome ones."

Celeste popped a whole cracker into her mouth. "Yeah, Ma, but this is the only one I can ever remember."

Mrs. Patel put her briefcase on the floor and bent to massage one stockinged foot. "Part of what Karva Chauth celebrates is friendship. Between women. And the smell of that soup is driving me crazy. A bit of sensitivity, please!"

"Sorry!" They all put their hands flat over their bowls.

"When Daddy gets here we'll go look for the moon. Bridge, do you want a lift home?"

"Sure," Bridge said. "That'd be great."

"I'll come too!" Tab said. "I love moon hunting."

Half an hour later, they trailed down the block after Tab's parents, who walked arm in arm to their car. Tab's father carried a plate covered with foil. It had been one of those weird chilly days that gets warmer as it goes on, and it was now just a tiny bit cool out.

"Your parents are really in love, aren't they?" Bridge asked Tab.

"I guess so," Tab said. "Sure."

"It's nice."

Tab looked at her. "Well, yours are too, right?"

"Sure. But you know that stuff Emily said last year, about her parents and the nine thousand things? It doesn't seem like that could happen to your parents."

"You think it could happen to yours?"

"I guess not. I don't know." She was thinking of Sherm's grandparents. How many of the nine thousand things could be waiting to surprise you after fifty years?

"Well, nobody *knows*," Tab said.

The car was small and the backseat smelled like nail polish remover. Tab's father put the plate down carefully between the two front seats. Bridge and Tab each took a window so they could look out for the moon.

"High ground or low buildings," Tab's mother said firmly. "That's what we need."

Her father turned the key in the ignition. "I know a place."

They drove with the windows open, stopping for lights, making slow turns, until Tab's father said "There!" and Bridge leaned out her window and saw the moon, a pale white sliver.

They pulled into an empty spot next to a fire hydrant. They were on a narrow street of low brownstones, with the moon sitting just above them. Bridge felt quiet pour into the car through the open windows, along with the smell of a fire from someone's backyard.

Tab looked at Bridge and scrunched up her nose. "I smell burnt marshmallows," she whispered.

Bridge inhaled, then smiled. "I love that smell." She heard laughter through the window of the nearest brownstone, and what sounded like a metal spoon scraping a pot, getting the last little bit from the bottom.

Tab's father looked at her mom. "Ready?" He picked up the plate and carefully began to take the foil off.

"Wait!" Tab's mom grabbed her purse from between her feet, unzipped it, and pulled out a small metal sieve. She held the sieve up to her face and looked at the moon through it. Then, with the sieve still to her eye, she turned and looked at Tab's father. She spoke a few words to him in French.

He answered her in French. Then he leaned over, pulled her hand down from her face, kissed her quickly, and held a water bottle out to her. She drank. And drank. And drank. Then she took a deep breath and said, "Food!"

Bridge and Tab were silent while he fed her with his

fingers—a piece of bread and then a piece of meat from the foil-covered plate. Darkness was falling quickly, and their faces blurred into silhouette.

After a minute, Tab's mom took the plate from her father. "These poor girls," she said between bites of food, "are probably bored to death."

As they pulled away into the street, Bridge inhaled again, filling herself with the scent of burnt marshmallow. She put her head close to Tab's and whispered, "That was intense."

"I know!" Tab's voice was loud, and it broke the spell that had been cast over all of them. Her parents started talking about regular things, their days at work.

"It didn't seem sexist, really," Bridge told Tab a minute later. "It just seemed nice."

For once, Tab said nothing. She just smiled into the dark.

VALENTINE'S DAY

The Bean Bar is hot lava: Mr. Barsamian totally knows you—and your parents.

But he would definitely let you have a bagel if you said you forgot your money. Maybe even one of those mango smoothies. You could always tell him it's a half day at your high school. Jamie goes to one of those competitive schools that are an hour away by subway, so he would have no way of knowing that you're lying.

You peek through the window. No Mr. Barsamian.

Instead, there's that blonde with the dreadlocks behind the register. She's been around for a few months, but you don't really know her because you don't come to the Bean Bar as much as you did in middle school. You walk in.

When you start telling the blonde about how you have no money but you're kind of a friend of the family, she smiles.

"Friend of the family. You know, I hear that a lot."

"Really?" You aren't sure what she means.

"Really." Those dreads are kind of fierce. Her T-shirt has a picture of two boxing gloves on it.

She puts her fists on her hips. "You realize this is a business, right?"

Oh. "Yes, I totally get that, and I'm going to pay. I could bring the money tomorrow."

She looks at you, dubious.

"Or even later today." You glance at a middle-aged woman in a red wool hat who's sitting at the closest table, definitely within earshot. This is embarrassing. "I could bring the money today," you tell the blonde.

"Excuse me. Are you all right?" The woman in the red hat is looking at you like she can see your brain and read everything in it.

You turn to her. "I'm fine." But your voice is suddenly bubbling with wetness. Anyone who knows you would know you're not all right.

"How old are you?"

"Fourteen."

Why did you say fourteen? You should have said seventeen. The guy at the copy shop thought you were in college. "It's a half day," you add, which just makes you sound stupid.

Her forehead wrinkles up. "And you're hungry? You have no money?"

You clear your throat, pull yourself together. "Actually, my friend is meeting me here." You throw your shoulders back. "She has money."

"Oh." Her eyes sweep over you, up and down, taking in clothes, shoes, nail polish, the turquoise bracelets that you and Gina bought one Saturday.

"All right," she says, suddenly smiling. "Just checking." And she leaves.

You turn back to the blonde behind the register. You've

now told two different stories: *I can pay tomorrow* and *I'm waiting for my friend with money*. She raises an eyebrow at you.

You give the door an impatient look, as if you wish your nonexistent friend would hurry up and get here.

"Aw, I'm just messing with you," the blonde says. "What can I get you? You ever try this halvah? It's Armenian. Full of protein."

Five minutes later, you're at a corner table with a toasted bagel. You could probably sit here all day, just a few blocks from home, and no one would know where to find you. You look out the window and sip your water.

You didn't have the nerve to ask for the smoothie.

Sometimes your body feels like a cage for all the stuff inside. You paint your nails, braid your hair, and buy the right kind of jeans, but none of it is really about you. That guy with the spiky hair at the copy shop looked like one kind of person, but he could have been anyone. And Vinny still looks like Vinny, the same girl who carefully wrapped bags of M&M's at her kitchen table while her grandmother sweated in front of the television and you floated in a lake in New Hampshire. She's the same person who ran to your apartment when she was eleven with a filthy kitten shoved down the front of her coat, begging you to take it. She'd found it trembling under a car on 105th Street and spent an hour coaxing it out.

"Why don't you take him to your house?" you'd said while it lurched around on your kitchen floor.

"She's a girl, dummy." Vinny got milk out of your fridge and poured some into a dish. "You have to take her. Please!

You know my dad doesn't do animals. I'm afraid they'll kill her at the shelter if no one wants her."

"What if my parents say no?"

"They won't."

An hour later, your dad came home with your sister to find you alone, crying over the kitten, whose belly had swollen to the size of a kickball. He called a vet and you rushed over together in a cab. She had worms and ear mites. And she was allergic to milk. But Vinny was right—your parents let you keep her.

You can see Vinny now, in homeroom, smiling as the Valentine's Day flowers are handed out. She always gets a bunch of them; she's still Snow White with a tan and a strut. But you don't know what's inside anymore.

FREEBIE

"This is blackmail!" Jamie shouted from the living room couch. "Blackmail!"

Jamie was always low on steps after track practice; he was usually starving, his knees were killing him from crawling, and no one else was home yet.

"Oh, it is not," said Bridge.

"Two dollars for cereal?" he cried.

"Cereal is annoying," Bridge told him calmly. "I have to go into the kitchen, open the box, get a bowl out. . . . This doesn't include your dishes, you know. If you want a bowl and spoon washed, it'll be another dollar."

Jamie let his head drop against the back of the couch and closed his eyes. "Fine. If you throw in some buttered toast. And you wash the plate after."

Bridge thought it over. Then she stuck out her hand, put on her best Rudolph voice, and said, "It's a deal!"

Jamie refused to shake. "No way. This is not a Hermey moment. Hermey is all about 'be yourself and follow your dream.' Hermey is *not* about 'blackmail your brother.' I won't let you use him that way."

She looked at him hopefully and said, "You can't fire me!

I quit!" It's what Hermey tells the chief elf, who's always putting Hermey down for wanting to be a dentist.

Jamie laughed. "Stop! All wrong!"

The doorbell rang. "I'll get it," Bridge told him. "No charge. You just relax."

She looked through the peephole. It was Alex. "It's your frenemy!" she called to Jamie.

"Well, let him in! Unless you charge for that. In which case he can just stand out there."

"He's wearing your Rolling Stones T-shirt," Bridge added, squinting.

"On second thought, lock the door."

"What's the official definition of 'blackmail'?" Bridge asked Alex when she had flung the door open.

"Using threats to get what you want," Alex told her. "Hello to you too."

"It ISN'T blackmail!" she told Jamie on her way to the kitchen to make his toast. "Look it up."

Opening the cereal box, Bridge heard Alex say, "You don't know what blackmail is?"

"Be quiet," Jamie said irritably.

"Have you told Bridge what you bet me?"

"I said be *quiet*," Jamie said. "Anyway, who says I'm going to lose?"

Alex smiled his condescending smile. Bridge couldn't see it, but she sensed it from the kitchen with perfect clarity. She opened the fridge and saw that her mom had been to the farmers' market—there was a bowl of green apples, Jamie's favorite. She reached for one and decided to throw it in for free.

BOLLYWOOD

"Okay, here goes: sock bun." Celeste raised her hairbrush and stood for a moment like the Statue of Liberty. She and Bridge were alone in the bedroom Celeste shared with Tab, who was scavenging costume parts in her parents' closet.

"I start by teasing my hair." Celeste flipped her head upside down, grabbed a thick handful of hair by the end, and started brushing it backward, toward her scalp.

Bridge watched, mesmerized, as Celeste moved from one section of her hair to another, brushing it all the wrong way. "Wow. It's like . . . a giant hair cloud."

"I know." Celeste's voice sounded different upside down. "Completely mental, right? Okay. Now"—she stood straight and reached for a hair band—"I just stick this whole mess into a big high pony."

Tab appeared in the doorway. "Celeste, can Em wear your outfit from Praveena's wedding?"

"Sure," Celeste said, tightening the base of her hair cloud into a ponytail. "That stuff will never fit me again."

"Thanks!" Tab clapped, gave a little jump, and disappeared.

Celeste produced what looked like a fat cotton bracelet.

"Okay, this is the sock part. See? I used a black one to match my hair. I cut the toe off and then rolled it up into a dough-nut like this. Now I just slip the end of my pony through the hole, and—watch."

She began to roll the sock doughnut up the length of her ponytail, folding her hair into it as she went, until all Bridge could see was a big circle of dark glossy hair.

"Cool," Bridge murmured.

"Yeah, brilliant, right?"

"Yeah. Brilliant."

When Celeste's giant hair roll reached the top of her ponytail, she grabbed another hair band and wrapped it around the base of the bun. "Some people use pins for the loose strands, but I don't. I like it a little bit messy."

"It looks really good." Celeste looked like a stylish balle-rina. "So what are you doing tonight?" Bridge asked her.

Celeste smiled. "I'm on trick-or-treat duty. There are a hundred kids in this building, and I swear they are the greedi-est things in New York. You have to watch them like a hawk or they'll clean you out before seven-thirty."

Bridge laughed.

"Now let's do you," Celeste said, waving her brush. "For the party!"

Bridge heard herself say, "Yeah. Okay."

An hour later, Bridge looked at herself in the mirror. She was wrapped in dark purple silk, with gold bangles on both wrists and black pencil around her eyes. The sock bun was perfect, she thought. Celeste had put it up high on her head and then pulled some long strands out to "frame her face." Bridge liked what she saw in the mirror more than she expected to and then was afraid that her own satisfaction would be obvious to everyone in the room. She frowned.

"You look super-pretty," Em said. "Try smiling."

Emily wore a wrapped dress like Bridge's, but hers had cut-outs at the waist that showed triangles of skin.

"I still don't understand how we went from superheroes to an Indian wedding party," Bridge said.

"Those superhero costumes were plastic kid stuff," Em said.

"And it's not a wedding party!" Tab said. "It's *Bollywood*."

"Right, Bollywood," Bridge said. "Whatever that is."

"I told you, it's like the Indian version of Hollywood. Which is cool." Em twirled in front of the mirror. Her phone chimed, and she ran over to it. "OMG. Look what Julie Hopper is wearing tonight." She held out the phone. "Get it? *Hopper?*"

Julie Hopper was wearing a bunny costume. A Playboy Bunny costume.

"What an idiot," Tab said. "She has a pom-pom on her butt!"

"It's *retro*," Em said. "A leotard and tights, big deal. And bunny ears. Which reminds me—no ears tonight, right, Bridge?"

Bridge grabbed her ears from Tab's bed and slipped them on.

"Bridge!" Tab and Emily exchanged a look.

Tab said, "You said you were going to wear them until Halloween, remember? This is Halloween."

"Right," Bridge said. "And therefore"—she adjusted the ears so that they fit exactly right—"I'm wearing them."

Tab rolled her eyes but was quiet. Bridge guessed that she was telling herself to put a pin in it.

Em had turned back to the mirror. "I don't get why the school party is for seventh graders only. It should be seventh and eighth together."

"It's probably so we don't get corrupted by people who stick pom-poms on their butts," Tab said. "Personally, I'm grateful."

"The eighth graders have the spring dance," Bridge said. "Before graduation."

Celeste walked in wearing sweats and a T-shirt. "The spring dance was so much fun," she said. "I can't believe that was only six months ago. Wow. Seems like so much longer."

"Yeah, we all know you're in high school now, Celeste." Tab looked her sister up and down. "I thought you were going out. Don't you have that party?"

"Nah," Celeste said. "I decided to hang here." She plopped down on one of the beds and ripped open a mini-Snickers.

Tab handed Bridge a few more gold bangles and said, "Don't lose these."

"Celeste, take a picture of us!" Em held out her phone. "I want to show Julie what we're wearing!"

U-TURN

The next day, Bridge sat alone backstage in the auditorium, hunched over her phone. Were those footsteps? She shoved her phone into her pocket and listened, squinting through the backstage gloom at the heavy red velvet curtain. She didn't know yet whether Mr. Partridge was the type to confiscate a phone. Half the teachers just pretended not to see them.

No one was coming, she decided. She pulled her phone out and looked again at the picture Em had posted—the one Celeste took of the three of them before they'd left for the party. Bridge stared at herself: at her long hair bundled on top of her head with strands escaping, at her penciled eyes looking dark and huge, at her arms inside the tangles of thin bracelets. She had never seen herself like this before.

She could wake up every morning and put on eye makeup, the way Em did. She could do more with her hair and wear something other than T-shirts. But she knew she wouldn't—that stuff would feel like more of a costume than the one she'd worn last night.

She made the picture bigger and moved it with her

thumb, panning across their three faces. Em's was serious, lips slightly puckered, head tilted. Bridge had to wonder if it was a look she practiced at home. Bridge's face looked, yes, undeniably pretty but also slightly stunned: eyes wide, face blank under the automatic smile. On Em's other side was Tab, sticking out her tongue and making peace signs with both hands. She was the only one who looked like herself, Bridge decided.

She paged down and read the comments again.

Gorgeous.

Prettiest girls in the seventh grade.

OMG. HOT!

There were twenty-six comments. And Em had taken the time to respond to every one of them: *Thanks!* Or *Aw, UR Nice*.

Julie Hopper had written *SO BOOTYFUL!! LOL*.

And Em had written back *ILYSM*.

The last comment on Em's page was from Patrick.

Your turn.

Beneath it was Em's response:

Soon.

And underneath that she'd added: ☺.

"Hey," a voice said. "You all alone back here?"

Sherm had sneaked up on her. He held the stage curtain open just slightly, so she could only see half of his smile.

"Yeah," Bridge said quickly, shoving her phone into her book bag. "We had a math sub. She let us out early."

She liked the way she and Sherm sort of *recognized* each other. Ever since the first intruder drill, Bridge had looked for him—in the halls, the school lobby, the cafeteria. Everywhere. And the more she looked, the more he seemed to be there.

"It's kind of dark," he said, glancing around. They were surrounded by folding chairs, music stands, and painted scenery from last year's spring play. "Is there a light switch?"

"Yeah, but I'm afraid to touch that thing." She pointed toward the light board, a gray metal box perched on a rolling metal cart against the back wall.

Sherm walked over to it, his hands in his pockets, and gazed at the rows of black switches. "So were you at the famous party last night?"

"Yeah, were you? I didn't see you."

Sherm shook his head. "Nope. How was it?"

"Everyone stood around talking to whoever they came with. Some people jumped up and down on the dance floor, which was really just a corner of the gym marked off with black masking tape. Stale cookies. How come you didn't go?"

He shrugged. "No date." After a beat, he added, "Just kidding."

When Sherm said "date," Bridge's head buzzed the same way it did when Madame Lawrence pointed at her in French class.

Sherm said, "I like this place when no one's here." He walked toward the bunched velvet curtain and stroked it with two fingers. "Cozy. And it smells like a woodshop."

"Yeah. It doesn't feel like school. You know? It feels kind of like a secret."

They heard a door bang open on the other side of the

curtain, followed by loud voices and clomping feet—the rest of the Wednesday tech crew. Bridge smiled. "Not that big a secret, I guess."

"If tech meets on Mondays and Wednesdays," Sherm said, "I wonder what it's like here at lunchtime on a Tuesday or a Thursday."

"It's probably exactly like this. Empty."

"Let's find out."

"When?"

"Tomorrow?"

Bridge shrugged. "Okay. Sure."

A hand appeared through the curtains and forcefully swept one aside so that it rolled a bit, making a wide opening.

"Ah." Mr. Partridge raised his eyebrows at them. He went to the gray metal box and flipped a switch, and suddenly everything was bathed in light. He flipped another switch and the light got brighter. "There," he said, smiling at Bridge and Sherm. "Sunshine."

"Got any candy wrappers?" Tab asked Bridge at recess. They were watching the soccer team's "informal practice," which was taking up most of the yard. Emily flew back and forth in her yellow sweatshirt.

"Wrappers?" Bridge repeated.

"From Halloween." Tab pulled a ziplock bag out of her jacket pocket. Inside were a few candy wrappers. "I'm collecting them for the Human Rights Club."

"So that's what the Human Rights Club does?"

Tab gave her a serious look. "Bridge. Do you know how

much foil gets thrown away every Halloween? It's like a million football fields of foil. If we keep wasting all our resources, there won't be any humans left to *have* rights."

Bridge put both hands up. "Okay! I'll bring some in tomorrow." Bridge didn't say what she was thinking: what about all the plastic bags the Human Rights Club was using to carry the candy wrappers around?

"Thanks." Tab stuffed the bag back into her pocket. "And for your information, the Human Rights Club is studying civil disobedience. Like Rosa Parks. The wrappers are just a side project."

The soccer ball rolled toward them. Tab bent down to grab it, then flung it back onto the field, where a swarm of yellow sweatshirts ran after it.

"Want a peppermint patty?" Tab said.

"Sure."

Tab handed her two. "We have all this candy left over. I kind of wonder whether Celeste even answered the door last night. I've eaten like half a bag already."

"Your poor teeth," Bridge said.

"Please. My teeth have bigger problems."

"Oh yeah. When's the big day?"

"Not for a while. Don't talk about it."

"You brought it up."

"Four teeth! Who has to get four teeth pulled, just for braces?" Tab held out a hand for Bridge's candy wrapper.

Bridge's dentist had told her mom that her mouth was too "immature" for braces. She'd probably have to wear them in high school, when everyone else had already gotten theirs off.

Bridge scanned the yard for Sherm and spotted him at the far end, standing against the fence with a few other kids. She watched him until Tab gave a big "Woot!" and butted her shoulder-to-shoulder. Em had scored a goal.

"Go, Emily!" Bridge shouted to make up for the fact that she'd missed it.

Em threw both arms up in the air, did a graceful U-turn, and started running back to her team.

SHERM

November 3

Dear Nonno Gio,

I hate Halloween now. Nonna gave me some of your navy stuff, but when I put it on, the jacket was huge and I looked like a little kid in grown-up clothes. I said I wasn't going to the party.

She said I should just go, and if I wasn't having fun I could leave. I told her I had a nauseous headache. Obviously that was a lie, but Nonna got me a cold washcloth for my neck and asked me if I wanted to lie down. We ended up watching a movie. Nonna left the candy on the stoop for trick-or-treaters.

It's hard to believe October 31 used to be my favorite day of the year. Remember when you were Tintin and I was your dog, Snowy? I still have that dumb wig you wore.

I probably should have gone to the party. I could have just worn my navy turtleneck with your old hat. The hat almost fits.

Sherm

P.S. Three months and eleven days until your birthday.

P.P.S. I decided to ask Mr. Partridge if I can learn the stage lights.

CHICKEN

"Chicken?" Bridge repeated. She and Em were in homeroom, sitting in the back row. She was thinking at first of the *bird* chicken.

"Yeah," Em said. "Chicken. You know. The whole thing with Patrick?"

"I *don't* know. What does Patrick have to do with chicken?"

"The game, dummy. Chicken? Like two cars drive directly toward each other until one chickens out and swerves away?"

"That's a game?"

"So I took that picture of my foot, right? And he sent me his ankle. I sent my leg, and he sent his belly button, blah blah blah."

"Wait—'blah blah blah'? What does that mean?"

Em rolled her eyes up to the ceiling. "I sent him a picture of my—thigh, I guess? I was wearing shorts and I wrote . . . something on it." She cut her eyes back to Bridge. "I didn't tell you guys. Sorry. I didn't want to hear Tab's lecture."

"You wrote on your leg? Like on your *skin*? What'd you write?"

"Um . . ." Em leaned in. "I wrote *Make me crazy*."

"Seriously?"

"I know. Julie Hopper and I were hanging out after

practice. It seemed really funny—we actually couldn't stop laughing."

" '*Make me crazy*'?"

"Shhh! It was Julie's idea, okay? And after that, he sent—this." She passed Bridge her phone under the table.

Bridge found herself looking at a head-to-toe picture of Patrick standing in his underwear. He had taken the picture in a mirror.

"Is this—real?" It wasn't as if Bridge hadn't seen Jamie in his boxers a thousand times. But still, this felt semi-*un*real.

Em nodded slowly, her face bright.

"Whoa," Bridge said. "When did he send this?"

"On Halloween. A lot of the eighth graders were at Julie's house watching horror movies."

"He took this picture at Julie's house?"

"Yeah. In the bathroom. According to Julie."

"But now you're going to stop, right? It's all . . . crazy!"

"I can't stop now!"

"Why not?"

"'Cause then I'm the chicken!"

"So what? The chicken is the smart one!"

"Julie says this goes on all the time. It's not a big deal. Okay?"

"*Okay?*" Bridge repeated. "What does 'okay' mean?" Bridge's brain flicked to all of those comments between Em and Julie: *UR gorgeous. ILYSM.*

"They're all in love with him, you know," Em said. "The girls on soccer. Do you even get how crazy it is that he picked me?"

"Em, lots of people would pick you."

"It's like a trust thing."

"A trust thing? You showed me his picture. You think he won't show people your picture?"

"I'm going to lose him if I don't, Julie says."

"*Julie* says? Em. Are you sure you even like him that much?"

Em just gave her a look. "Please help me, Bridge. I want the picture to be decent. Not one of those stupid selfies."

"I *am* helping you. I'm helping by saying *stop*."

"You know what? You have no idea. You just—don't. Bridge, I kissed him."

"When?"

"Right after Halloween."

"*Halloween?* That was days ago! You didn't tell us?"

"I know. I should have."

"Did you tell Julie?"

Em looked at her desk. "We were at practice together. It just came up."

"Wow. So it 'came up' with Julie, but not with *us?*"

"I said I'm sorry. I didn't know if you guys would even, like, want to know."

"Of course I'd want to know! This is a big deal, Em. Right?"

Em nodded. "Right."

"What was it like?"

"Good. Weird. Good."

"Let's find Tab," Bridge said. "As soon as the bell rings."

"Tab's all *judgy* now, with the Berperson."

"She cares about you."

"I know. But neither of you gets it."

Bridge looked at Em. "Maybe I don't get *everything*, but look—we're sticking together. Okay? We're still a set." She grabbed Emily's hand.

"So you'll help me with the picture? Please? Please-please?"

"But you're not going to rush into this, right? You have to promise." She squeezed Em's hand. "Don't send any more pictures until you think about it."

"I promise. You're the best. Can you come over right after school tomorrow?"

"Tomorrow?"

"Just to take the picture. I won't send it. Promise." Em hesitated. "And don't tell Tab, okay?"

The two-minute bell rang, and Bridge's attention jerked to the blank page in front of her. "Can I look at your French homework?"

Emily smiled. "Sure."

After the last bell, Bridge was bumping along in the sea of kids leaving the building when Em grabbed her arm. "Hey, superstar."

"Hey. Where were you before sixth period? Tab and I waited by your locker."

"Nowhere. Everywhere."

Bridge looked at Em more closely. "What's that supposed to mean?"

Em put her mouth next to Bridge's ear. "What would you say if I told you I just kissed Patrick in the hall behind the science lab?"

"Congratulations, I guess?" But Bridge couldn't exactly

picture it. Did they just stand there in the hall with their lips touching, or did they lean up against the wall? What did they do with their hands? And weren't they afraid someone would see them?

Em smiled. "Thanks. Gotta go. Banana Splits." Em rubbed her stomach theatrically and started walking backward toward the library, bumping into everyone in her way.

"Save me a cookie?" Bridge called.

"Not a chance!" Em yelled.

VALENTINE'S DAY

The blond girl with dreadlocks is wiping down tables. You can now see that her boxing-glove T-shirt has words on the back: TOUCH ME AND YOUR FIRST LESSON IS FREE.

You try not to meet her eyes, but there aren't that many places to look.

"So what happened to your money?" she asks from across the room.

You think about saying that your bag was stolen. "I forgot it. At home."

"You need to call someone?"

"No, I'm fine."

"You got a phone?"

"Yeah. But not with me."

"You left that at home too?"

"Yeah."

"You must have left in a hurry."

You say nothing to that.

"How old are you?"

"Seventeen."

"You told the lady in the goofy hat that you're fourteen." She gives you a hard look and then walks back behind the register, where she yanks a gigantic purse onto the counter and starts feeling around inside. "You can use my phone."

"Thanks. But I'm really just waiting for my friend."

"Your friend," she says.

"Right." You want to change the subject. "So, how do you like working here? It's been a while, right?"

She nods. "Five months. It's pretty good. Nice boss, free food, can't complain. Do you have a job?"

"Not really. I mean, I babysit."

"I used to babysit. My brothers. But I never got paid."

"Oh. That sucks."

"I'm Adrienne," she says, and sticks her hand out.

You have to get up and walk over to her to shake. Her grip is slightly painful. She shoves her bag back underneath the counter and then starts hopping from foot to foot. You are not about to ask why.

"So." She glances around. "Do you really know the Barsamians, or was that just something to say?"

"No, I do. Our families are friends. I remember when Mr. Barsamian bought this place, after Bridge—that's his daughter—"

Adrienne nodded. "I know Bridge."

"Well, she got hit by a car, about five years ago."

Adrienne blinked, stopped jumping. "Huh. I didn't know that. Was it bad?"

"Really bad. She was in the hospital a lot, having these surgeries. Anyway, that's when her dad opened this place. Before that, he had a different job—he traveled a lot, I think."

"What about the brother?"

"Jamie?"

"Yeah."

"Jamie's great. I mean, we don't hang out much or anything. He's a year ahead of me, and we don't go to the same high school."

"I don't miss high school."

"Yeah."

"I left early."

"You did?"

Adrienne nodded. "I'm doing this boxing thing. And working."

"Wow. My parents would flip."

Adrienne smiled. "Mine definitely flipped. They want me to be a marine biologist. I'm thinking about it."

"Wouldn't you have to finish high school for that?"

"Oh, I did finish. Got my last credits at summer school and skipped senior year. Who needs the drama, right?"

"Yeah."

"So now I'm into boxing. Maybe I'll go to college next year, maybe I'll wait. You can have it all, but you can't have it all at once."

You look at her. "How old are you?"

She laughs. "How old are *you*?"

"Almost fifteen," you admit.

She nods, then points at herself. "Eighteen."

"You look older."

"You don't. You sure you don't want to use my phone?"

"No thanks. I should go. I guess my friend isn't coming."

But you just sit there.

"Keep me company for a while," Adrienne says. "I get bored."

SUITS

What Emily had decided to do was take a picture of herself in her new jeans, with no shirt on.

"But wearing a bra, which is basically the same as a bathing suit," she told Bridge. "And I'll do one of those photo filters, so it's kind of fuzzy? You know, artsy."

"Tell me again why you're doing this?" Bridge said. "One more time."

"What if my boyfriend asked for a picture of me in my bathing suit?"

"I'd say he was creepy. Is Patrick even your boyfriend?"

"You promised not to be judgy. People walk around the city in less than a bathing suit!"

"I'm not being judgy," Bridge said. "I'm being—asky."

Em started brushing her hair out in front of the mirror. "We want to, like—show ourselves. Be real. Do things for each other we wouldn't do for anyone else."

"Why don't you just talk to each other? Isn't that more real, more *you*, than a fuzzy picture of your bra?"

"I think," Em said, "that you're, like, just not there yet. With Sherm."

"Sherm! What are you talking about?"

"And Tab . . . Tab has no idea *at all*."

"She turned you down, didn't she? You asked her for help and she said no. Right?"

Em mimicked: "'You know I love you, but I can't be part of this.'"

"She does love you."

"I *know*. I love her too."

But suddenly the air felt different. Tab wasn't here with them, on purpose. That had never happened before.

"Let's get this over with," Bridge said.

Em put her brush down, crossed her arms, and pulled her T-shirt over her head in one quick motion. Underneath, she was wearing a lacy black bra.

"Wow, fancy," Bridge said. "Where'd you get that?"

"My mom's drawer. Can you believe it? She has, like, ten of these."

"You can wear your mom's bras?"

"Shut up."

"You look like a perfume ad or something."

Em smiled. "Really?"

On her way home, Bridge stopped by the Bean Bar. It was one of their busy times, right after the end of the regular workday.

"Bonjour, Finnegan!" Adrienne said, waving to Bridge over the customers' heads.

Her dad looked up. "You okay, honey?"

"Yeah. Just saying hi."

"Did something happen?"

"No, Dad—I told you, I'm just saying hi." Nothing had

happened, she told herself. Emily promised not to send any of the pictures they took. Bridge had made her swear, twice, that she wouldn't do anything yet.

"It's dark already," her father said. "I'll walk you home."

"I'm fine!" Bridge said, turning around. "It's only five blocks. I can walk myself."

Of course she could. She'd walked home alone in the dark before. But once she left the Bean Bar, Bridge couldn't remember exactly *when* she'd walked home alone in the dark before.

She decided to count her steps. Jamie was right: she took about a hundred steps for every block she walked. When she got to her building, she was on step 485. She wondered if she could make it to her room without going over five hundred. She glanced around and took four giant steps to the elevator. It reminded her of that game, Mother, May I? She used to play it with Jamie in the hallway of their apartment.

You may take two giant steps.

Mother, may I?

Yes, you may.

In her mind's eye, Bridge could see Jamie, hair in his eyes, wearing the Spider-Man pajamas he loved all the way through fourth grade. That intense look he used to get when he was trying to do something hard.

She reached her room on step 498. Then she went and knocked on Jamie's door.

"Enter!" Jamie was hunched over his math homework. Bridge could see graph paper.

"What'd you bet Alex?" she said. "Come on, tell me."

He pointed his pencil at her and said, "I told you, it's irrelevant."

"If you tell me, I'll make you soup. For free."

Jamie hestitated.

Bridge smiled at him.

Then he said, "No deal."

SHERM

Sherm loved the feeling inside his house after his parents left for work.

He and his grandmother both woke early, but they stayed out of the way until the questioning mumble of his parents' first movements became the sound of running water, quick heels on the wooden floors, a spike or two of laughter. And then: urgency in their voices, someone always rushing back upstairs for one last forgotten something, until finally—kiss, kiss, love you!—the door slammed behind them.

It was as if Sherm and his grandmother supported themselves while a windstorm blew through the house every morning and—kiss, kiss, love you!—left through the front door. Then the house seemed to exhale. Sherm became aware of the sound of the radio in the kitchen and the smell of his grandmother's coffee, and beneath that, he felt his grandmother's satisfied presence, which never changed.

He always sat at the kitchen table and did his math homework while she cooked his breakfast and wrapped up his lunch for school. She never had the appearance of hurrying, and yet things were done quickly.

Sherm used math homework to wake up his brain. When

he didn't have any, he missed it. Writing out each problem, going through the steps, circling his answers—it was a satisfying system check. He was like a pilot in his cockpit.

His grandmother never asked him what he wanted for breakfast. She put an omelet in front of him, with toast grilled on the stove with olive oil, or semolina pancakes, or a frittata with peppers and mushrooms. After she put down his plate, he thanked her, and she rested her hand on his wrist for a few seconds, as if she were gently pressing something there—and then she walked to the sink or to her coffeepot. Even the morning after his grandfather left, she got up and did this for him, never letting her eyes stray to the chair across from Sherm's.

This morning it was French toast. No syrup: his grandmother used powdered sugar. Next to his plate, she put a small bowl of blueberries. He ate, thinking about everything and nothing. Thinking about Bridge.

Using the side of his fork, Sherm cut up his last piece of French toast. He made it into a face with two pointy, lopsided ears on top, using blueberries for eyes.

The guys at school had started calling her his girlfriend. She was definitely not his girlfriend. But she might be his best friend.

Sherm got along with everyone—he was like that. But once his grandfather left, Sherm realized that with the guys at school, talking was like a game where everyone piled on jokes and the winner was the person whose joke ended up on top. With girls, it was a different game, a lot of teasing and trading fake insults. But it wasn't that way with Bridge.

When he finished eating, Sherm brought his plate to the sink, jumped up the steps to the second floor of the house, ran down the short hallway to his room, and grabbed a pack of cards from where he'd left them on his desk. Then he ran back down the stairs to the kitchen to pick up his backpack and hug his grandmother, breathing her kitchen smell—it would have to hold him through the long day—and left.

He could only imagine how quiet the house was after that.

After his grandfather left, Sherm's parents blew through the house a little more quietly for a while. They were stunned.

They kept saying it, on the phone, or to each other: "Stunned."

People's parents got divorced, but whose *grandparents* got divorced? Officially, Sherm's father was the kid going through it, only he wasn't a kid. He was a cardiologist.

After a while, though, things went back to normal, except that Sherm's grandfather was gone. His grandmother left all the pictures of him right where they were, on the walls and the tabletops. It was almost as if he'd died and they were trying not to forget him. But he hadn't died. He still texted Sherm at least three times a week. And Sherm couldn't forget him anyway.

Sherm was a block from school when his phone buzzed. He slid it from his pocket. A text. Not from his grandfather. No words. Just a picture.

A WARM OBJECT

"The *weirdest* thing happened," Tab said, poking the crusts of her sandwich into her thermos. "So it's like five in the morning, and suddenly I'm wide awake, which is weird, and for some weird reason I'm thinking *something's weird.*"

"Sounds . . . weird," Sherm said.

Tab pointed a warning finger at him. "Don't make fun of me, Sherman."

He smiled. "Sorry." He looked at Bridge. "Ready to spit?"

"Wait," Bridge said, still straightening the cards in her hand. "Not yet."

In a few short weeks, backstage had become a place that was theirs, a secret corner carved out of the great un-ownable space called school.

Tab started again. "Anyway, it's dark, right? And I sit up, and something *drops into my lap*. At first I thought it was Sashi, but that would be weird because Sashi always, *always* sleeps with Celeste."

"In her bed, you mean?" Scrolling through her texts, Em pretended to shudder. "Evan says you should never let a cat watch you sleep."

"Well, that's just ignorant," Tab said.

"Tell it to Evan. He says they can steal your breath. Or your soul or something."

"Listen!" Tab said. "So I touch this thing in my lap and it's like—this warm object that feels just like human flesh."

"Ugh!" Bridge said.

"Guess what it was," Tab said.

"What?" Em said.

"It was my *arm*. My own arm! Dead asleep so that I couldn't feel it from the inside. My arm was like this random skin-covered object that fell on me! When I touched it, it was just like touching someone *else's* arm. How weird is that? I can't even tell you how weird."

Bridge looked at the fat deck of cards Sherm held while he took double bites of his sandwich. "Hurry up," she said. "You're messing with my momentum. This is the part where I crush you."

"One-two-three *spit*." They each slapped a card onto the floor. Then their hands flew, throwing cards on top of cards until Bridge yelled "Out!" and banged her hand down on the smaller of the two spit piles.

She smiled at Sherm and began straightening the cards into a thin, tight pack. Fewer cards meant she was winning, and she liked to win. But she never liked the feeling of just a few cards in her hand.

When Sherm wasn't looking, Bridge finger-combed her hair over the sides of the cat-ears headband.

When she'd shown up for school wearing the cat ears on November 1, Em had called a meeting in the fourth-floor bathroom, which was almost always empty.

"Halloween was yesterday," Tab had said firmly. "You're still wearing the ears. Are you going to wear them forever? If you're going to wear them forever, you should tell us."

"Why?" Bridge asked.

"Because." Em looked at herself in the mirror and blew the bangs out of her eyes. "Then maybe Tab will stop asking me what I think it means."

"I don't know what it means," Bridge said. "I just know they feel good."

Tab and Em glanced at each other. "There's nothing you're not telling us?" Tab said.

Bridge laughed. "Like what?"

"To tell you the truth, I like them now," Em said.

Tab leaned away and looked at Bridge. "I guess they are kind of a 'statement.'" She used air quotes.

"Great," Bridge said. "Then let's put a pin in it. A really big pin."

The truth was that Bridge didn't even think about the cat ears anymore, unless a little kid pointed at her on the street or some jerk said something obnoxious. Tab's mom said that when people reached out to hurt your feelings, it was because *they* secretly felt *they* deserved to be talked to that way. She said that they had "long, hard roads ahead" and that you should just wish them well. Bridge didn't examine the idea too closely because she liked it and hoped, really hoped, that it was true about the long, hard roads.

Although she wasn't so sure about the wishing-them-well part.

. . .

Tab shoved her lunch bag into her backpack. "The whole dead-arm thing was way weirder than it sounds. I might even write a reflection about it, for the Berperson."

"But there's no important feminist message!" Em said.

"Ha, ha," Tab said, unwrapping a butterscotch.

"Sure there is," Bridge said. "She experienced her body as an object!"

Even Tab laughed. "She's gonna love it." She glanced at Em, who was texting again. "Did you even eat anything?"

Em shook her head. "Too nervous. I can never eat before I sing. You aren't nervous?"

Tab jumped experimentally, landing with flat-footed thuds on the stage. "Nope."

"Lucky," Em said.

Emily hadn't said a word about the pictures since the afternoon Bridge had helped her take them almost a month before. Bridge had pretty much stopped worrying.

When the Talentine show audition notices were passed out, Em had been scornful. "It's like they're always trying to control us—that's what Julie Hopper says. So we have a dance on Halloween that keeps us out of trouble, and we have a talent show for Valentine's Day to distract everyone from the fact that half of us are total geeks."

Bridge had wondered about Em's definition of a total geek.

"Or," Tab had said, "it's just a fun show. I notice you're still trying out."

"Yeah, well, if it's where everyone is going to be, I guess I want to be there too. And if you've got a voice, you might as well use it, right?"

Em sang. She sang really well. Tab juggled, not all that well, but a lot better than most people. She'd learned at the circus shed at sleepaway camp.

Auditions began right after last period.

"Performers only!" Mr. Partridge told the kids peeking in the auditorium-door windows. "No *gawking*!" And he knocked on the glass until they went away.

Every kid who wanted to audition got five minutes on-stage. A few of the eighth-grade Tech Crew kids helped plug in the amps and carry microphone stands.

The three audition judges were stationed just below the stage: the vice principal, Mr. Ramos; the head of the language department, Madame Lawrence; and Mr. Partridge, who stood at the light board, which he'd rolled out on its metal cart.

The rest of the tech crew was also there. Mr. Partridge had seated them on the left side of the auditorium, in the first two rows of seats. Bridge and Sherm sat next to each other and watched as the kids took turns performing.

How did people do it? Bridge wondered. Sing all alone in front of everyone? Or worse, *dance* in front of everyone? One girl, an eighth grader who played the piano, was shaking so hard she had to start four times. After the third mess-up she got up to leave, but all the kids waiting their turns cheered and clapped and wouldn't stop making noise until the girl, cheeks wet with tears, broke into a smile and sat down again. That time, she got through it.

Mr. Partridge was right, Bridge realized. This place was different from every other room in the school.

Still, sitting there, she was getting more and more nervous for Em and Tab. She felt almost light-headed when Tab's name was finally called.

She elbowed Sherm. "Here goes nothing," she whispered.

"Stop worrying." Sherm had his notebook out. He'd sketched a neat diagram of the light board and was watching Mr. Partridge flip switches. Occasionally Sherm circled something on his diagram, or wrote a question to himself. It was kind of adorable, Bridge thought.

"He's going to teach you all that," Bridge reminded him. "You don't have to figure it out yourself."

"I know. I'm just getting a feel for it."

Tab grinned from the stage. She had two green apples in each hand, which she raised above her head with a flourish. Bridge waved and gave her a thumbs-up.

Tab's longest continuous juggle lasted about thirty seconds. She dropped most of her apples at some point, but finished nicely by holding one of them in her mouth while juggling the other three. Then, shifting her juggling to one hand, she took a dramatic bite from the apple in her mouth, made a face like it was sour, and threw it out to the first row, where someone caught it. Then she strolled off stage, juggling with two hands again. Everyone clapped and hooted and stomped. Bridge exhaled.

"See?" Sherm said. "She did great. That was hilarious."

When Em was called, she mounted the stage steps with her head down, glancing up only when she got to the big blue X taped to the middle of the stage floor.

She looked scared. This was not the same Em who had bounced around up there for the rock-paper-scissors tournament a couple of months before.

Bridge tried to give her a smile and a thumbs-up, but Em was looking at Mr. Partridge, who had stepped away from the light board to talk up at her. Bridge heard him say quietly, "Shoulders. Smile. Sing to the audience."

Em nodded, dropped her shoulders, forced a smile, and sang to the back wall.

Em's singing was powerful and sweet and it felt like something she was giving away. Her smile began to look real.

Bridge glanced at Sherm, who had stopped taking notes and was watching Em with a serious look.

Bridge whispered to Sherm. "She's good, right?"

"Yeah. She is."

Everyone went crazy when Emily finished. A couple of kids stood on their chairs and waved their phones back and forth like they were at a concert. Em hugged herself and ran down the steps to her seat. As Em passed, Bridge heard Mr. Partridge say, "Atta girl. That's the way to do it." And Em said, "Thanks, Mr. P."

Mr. P.

Mr. Partridge, Bridge realized, was Em's Mr. P. from the Banana Splits. How had she not known that?

"But next time," he called after Emily, "sing to the audience, not to the wall!"

Bridge felt a ping of jealousy. She had assumed that the Tech Crew kids were Mr. Partridge's favorites. But he never showed up at their meetings with black-and-white cookies from Nussbaum's. Compared to waiting in line at Nussbaum's, it was nothing to order up a couple of pizzas.

Tab texted Bridge that night:

Tab: Em is definitely in. She was one of the best. Maybe THE best.

Bridge: You were really good too! So funny!

Tab: But Em was amazing.

SHERM

November 28

Dear Nonno Gio,

I have a decision to make.

Have you ever heard the riddle about the two brothers standing in front of the two doors? One door leads to heaven, and the other one leads to hell, but you don't know which is which.

Thanksgiving was pretty terrible. The Philadelphia cousins brought apple pie and tried to pretend nothing was different. Mostly we watched football.

When you called before dinner (I could tell it was you from the way Mom's voice changed), I went straight into the bathroom and played games on my phone until I was sure you were gone.

Dad said grace before we ate the same way you always did, but then he made everyone say what they were thankful for. Later I found Na in her room, just sitting on the bed. I'm still getting your texts and chucking them.

People act like riddles are hard, but real life is harder. In real life, there are always more than two doors.

I guess I know what I'm going to do.

From,
Sherm

P.S. Two months, sixteen days until your birthday.

VALENTINE'S DAY

Adrienne has to get some napkins and stuff from the back room. She asks if you mind standing behind the register for a minute. "You know, so the place looks open."

You like standing behind the counter. It reminds you of playing store when you were a kid—you and your sister would line up a bunch of junk on the coffee table in the living room: plastic food from the toy kitchen, some Matchbox cars, a couple of action figures. Your parents would place their orders: spaghetti and meatballs, pancakes, a peanut-butter-and-honey sandwich.

You remember how your dad liked to ask for a pear-and-lettuce sandwich, how you'd always tell him you were all out of lettuce, and how every single time he would fall to the floor and pretend to cry, just to make you laugh.

You and Vinny and Zoe used to be the girls in the secret place at the top of the climbing tower with your legs stretched out in front of you and the soles of your feet pressed together to make a star. In middle school, you pooled your money most days after school and shared a slice of pizza and a Frappuccino three ways, giggling and taking turns with the straw. Now all of that feels just as imaginary as those pear-and-lettuce sandwiches.

Vinny wanted all eyes on her, all the time. She was the one who licked the poison berry juice off her fingers, the one who dared you to steal nail polish, the one who was obnoxious to the lady in the makeup store who told you no more free samples. But Vinny also made you feel as if you were exactly where you wanted to be, if not exactly who.

When you began to catch glimpses of something different—like that spoonful of cinnamon, and the smile that went along with it—you made excuses for her. That's Vinny, you told yourself. She doesn't really want to upset anyone. There's just that hurt part of her, like some kind of fire that always wants to be fed.

But another part of you, the part that stayed quiet, began to understand that maybe Vinny, your Vinny, was gone.

INTRUDERS

Sherm tapped Bridge on the shoulder as she was walking toward third period.

"Emily was looking for you," he said, his face worried. "I think she was crying."

"Where?" Bridge said.

Bridge ran to the auditorium, where she found Em sitting on the floor between rows, her back against a wall and her legs straight out in front of her. She wasn't crying. It was more like staring.

"What?" Bridge said. "What happened?"

Em looked up. "I think I did something really stupid."

It had been a weird morning: three kids were called down to the main office during social studies, and then in French they'd had the second intruder drill. Bridge thought that intruder drills belonged to the very small set of things that are even less fun than French.

"What happened?" Bridge said again.

Em inhaled. Em exhaled.

"Say something," Bridge said.

"You remember how last time, during the intruder drill, I

told you that everyone had to get in the coat closet, and Sara J. and Ellie both started crying?"

"Yeah."

Em took another breath, released it. "So this time, Ms. Madison says, we're supposed to play telephone."

Bridge shook her head. She didn't know the game. Whenever she discovered something that everyone besides her seemed to know, she assumed they had learned it during third grade, which she'd missed because of the accident.

"Telephone?" Em said. "Where someone whispers a message to the person next to him, and then that person whispers it to the next person? It's supposed to be funny because, like, people misunderstand what's being whispered, and then they say what they *thought* they heard, and the message gets all mangled."

"Em. What *happened*?"

"I'm getting to it. So David Marcel is next to me, he's practically standing on my feet in the stupid closet, breathing all over me, and the 'secret message' is coming down the line, and everyone is giggling and going 'Shhh!' really loudly. If we'd been hiding from a real gunman, we'd all be toast right now. Anyway, David leans away so Sara J. can whisper in his ear, and then he leans toward me and whispers, 'You're a slut.' And then he cracks up laughing, and stupid Eliza is on my other side going 'What is it? Come on!' She's practically shoving her ear into my mouth because she's so desperate to know."

And then, Emily said, she had busted out of the closet to run to the girls' bathroom, but the classroom door had been locked for the drill. So she stood there shaking the knob while the teacher patted her back and told her everything was okay, obviously thinking that Em had freaked about the nonexistent armed intruder, who was actually the last person on her mind.

When the drill finally ended, Ms. Madison sent Em to the school counselor with a note, but Em had just stuffed the note in her pocket and gone to the auditorium, where she found Sherm doing his English homework.

"David Marcel is an idiot," Bridge said. "I get that you didn't like it, but why are you this upset? He's always saying something idiotic."

"Something happened," Em said. "Something else."

Bridge carefully slid down the wall next to her. It was a tight squeeze. "What?"

"Those pictures we took? I sent one to Patrick. And—I guess he must have showed it to some people."

"You said you wouldn't do anything without telling me. You promised!"

Em shook her head in slow motion. "It's like that thing vampires have—glamour? They, like, turn it on you, and you can't resist, your brain goes fuzzy, and whatever they say seems so *right*. Do you know what I'm talking about? Do you know what that's like?"

"No," said Bridge. It sounded horrible, she thought. "Do you know how many people he showed it to?"

Emily shook her head. "No idea. I got two weird comments on my page this morning. I didn't recognize the names—"

She pulled her phone out of her bag and held it out to Bridge. Em's page was mostly soccer-team photos, plus a couple of shots of Sashi, Tab's cat. There had been two comments posted that morning.

The first one said UR HOT.

The second one said *CAN I HAZ MORE PICTURES?*

"I thought they were mistakes, like for someone else," Em said. "Or just—guys being random. But then when David Marcel . . ." She didn't finish the sentence.

"This might be kind of bad," Bridge said.

"It's definitely bad," Em said. "Absolutely, positively bad."

Bridge put a hand over one of Em's. "So it'll be a thing, a bad thing, but then it'll be over."

"David Marcel," Em said. "I can't believe David Marcel saw that picture."

Bridge was doing homework on her bed after dinner when she got a text from Tab:

CALL ME.

"Why do you text me to call you?" Bridge said when Tab answered her cell. "Why don't *you* just call *me?*"

"Emily told me what happened," Tab said. "I'm really mad, Bridge."

"Me too. I hate David Marcel. He's—"

"No, I'm mad at *you.*"

"Me?"

"How could you have helped Em take that picture? How?"

"Me? She was going to take a picture either way!"

"You don't know that. If we'd both said no, I bet she wouldn't have done it."

"She was *begging.* And I made her promise not to send it without talking to me. That was supposed to be part of the deal."

"Oh, I get it—so you were going to decide whether or not she should send it? You were, what, thinking it over?"

"That's not what I meant. I told her not to—fifty times!"

"And then you took the picture *for* her."

Bridge didn't say anything.

"Em is fragile, Bridge."

"Fragile? Which Em are you talking about?"

But Bridge knew the Em she was talking about. Tab meant the Em who sang to the wall while her legs shook. The Em who never talked about the Banana Splits unless she was bragging about the cookies. The Em who did whatever Julie Hopper told her to do. That Em.

"You're lucky we don't do fights," Tab said. "Because if we did, we'd be in a *big* fight right now!" And she hung up.

Tab had hung up on her. Bridge stared at her phone. Ten seconds later, a text popped up:

Love you. Still mad.

Bridge rolled to her back and stared at a small hole in her bedroom ceiling. There had been a screw there once, where a little metal bar hung above her head. She'd used it after the accident, to pull herself into a sitting position.

Her phone dinged again. A group text from Emily to her and Tab:

U guys up?

Tab's answer popped up right away: **Right here!**

Bridge typed: **Me too.**

Then she typed back to Tab on the other thread:

Love you too.

SHERM

November 29

Dear Nonno Gio,

I had the meeting with Mr. Ramos this morning. He's the vice principal. It was pretty bad. I had to name names. A couple of hours later, Emily came into the auditorium crying.

What if I just made things even worse?

I wish I could see what would have happened if I <u>hadn't</u> told. You told me once that every time a decision is made, the universe splits into two. So now there's a universe in which I kept my mouth shut. But I can't see what it looks like.

I guess that means that somewhere there's a universe in which you never left. I wonder what you're doing right now in that universe, whether you're sitting here with me in the kitchen. Na is making the almond biscotti. The house smells amazing. I wonder what it smells like in your universe.

Sherm

P.S. Two months, fifteen days.

VALENTINE'S DAY

Adrienne is wrapping yesterday's muffins. "Mr. Barsamian gives them to the soup kitchen on a Hundred and Fifteenth Street," she says. "You know they have a real chef there? He comes in sometimes."

You stand next to the industrial-size box of Saran Wrap, ripping off pieces and passing them to her. You still don't feel like talking, but it feels good to be doing something.

On the counter near the muffins is a small plastic figurine, a boy with a pointy hat, purple pants, and a big swoop of yellow hair. You can't imagine Mr. Barsamian owning such a thing.

"Is that yours?" You point.

"Yeah. It was a gift."

"What is it?"

She picks up the plastic guy and gives him a serious look. "I'm told it's an elf who wants to be a dentist."

You laugh. "He's perfect for you."

"How so?"

"Because you're a genius who wants to be a boxer?"

"Who said I'm a genius?"

"You finished high school a year early, right?"

"I went to summer school. I'm not a genius." Then she smiles. "Above average, definitely."

Gina would love that elf.

Adrienne stops your hand as you reach for the plastic wrap for the umpteenth muffin. "There are two banana-chocolate-chip muffins left," she says, looking serious. "It's possible that we should eat them. I mean, it *is* Valentine's Day." She squints at the window. "And I don't see anyone rushing to bring us any candy."

You laugh, then stop yourself. You know you shouldn't be having fun today.

You also know she's wondering why you're here.

Gina loves the word "umpteen." She says it's the best word ever. "Ask me to use it in a sentence," she'll say. And if you do, she always says the same thing: "Let's eat umpteen cookies." Only Gina would have a favorite word. Gina has a favorite everything.

A man comes into the Bean Bar, walks right up to you as if you belong there, and says, "Medium coffee and a blueberry-bran. Please."

Adrienne nods at you, and you grab a cup, pour the coffee, and point the guy to the lids and the milk. Adrienne hands him the muffin.

"Teamwork," she says when he's gone. She pats you on the back and hands you a banana-chocolate-chip muffin. She still doesn't ask.

BELLS

Bridge gave a fake stretch and tried to sound casual. "Hey, Simon got called down to the office during math this morning. Do you know why?"

"No," Sherm said, dealing the cards. "I don't even know Simon."

She yawned. The yawn was real: Em had texted Bridge and Tab steadily until one-thirty in the morning. Not about David Marcel, or Patrick, or the picture, but about everything else: television, her hair, music, her brother.

"That's weird," Bridge told Sherm, "because I asked him what's up, and he said, 'Ask your boyfriend.' I mean, obviously you're *not* my—"

"Obviously," Sherm said.

"But he meant you."

Obviously.

"So you don't know what's going on?" She looked at him. It was possible that Sherm had seen Em's picture by now. It was even possible that Sherm had been called down to the office himself. Was that what Simon had meant?

Sherm hesitated. "No."

Later, after knowing him a few more years, Bridge would

decide that one of her favorite things about Sherm was that he was a terrible liar.

He waved his cards. "Are we playing or what? The bell's going to ring pretty soon."

They heard footsteps—someone was crossing the stage on the other side of the heavy curtain. After a few seconds, Tab appeared, having punched her way through. Her hair was a static mess.

"I couldn't find the stupid opening! Bridge. Come! Em is freaking again."

Sherm followed them out.

Tab led them to the girls' bathroom on the fourth floor, where there were only a few classrooms. Sherm stopped outside, but Bridge said, "It's okay, no one's ever here," and pulled him in.

Em was sitting on the floor again, her back against the sink wall, her eyes on her knees, which were pulled up tight to her body. It made Bridge think of the first intruder drill and the way her English teacher had said "Make your bodies small!" It was only now, looking at Em all curled up, that Bridge got it: smaller bodies meant smaller targets.

"The school knows." Em's voice was completely flat. "And guess what? David Marcel didn't just *see* the picture. He had it on his phone. And he sent it to a bunch of people. Mr. Ramos is calling my mom tomorrow morning. He says I have tonight to tell her everything myself, if I want to."

"Oh, Em!" Tab and Bridge went to wrap their arms around her, sitting on the floor so that they could press against her from both sides. Sherm remained standing just inside the door.

Em was still staring at her knees.

"I should probably say something now," Sherm said.

"Say something to who?" Bridge said.

He took one step toward them, seemed to reconsider, and stopped. "I'm really sorry, Emily. I just—didn't know what to do."

Bridge began to tell him that he didn't know what he was talking about.

"Wait," Tab said. "What exactly are you sorry about, Sherman?"

His neck got red. "I'm the one who told Mr. Ramos about the picture. I had it on my phone—I mean, someone sent me a text. I just wanted it to stop."

"*You told?*" Tab yelled. "Like things weren't bad enough? What kind of human are you?"

"I was making it *less* bad!" Sherm said. Now his face was red too. "After I talked to Mr. Ramos, everyone got called down to the office and they all had to erase the picture. Mr. Ramos told them all this scary stuff like how they could go to jail. That's the only reason they stopped sending it all over the place!"

Em was crying now.

"Why didn't you tell me?" Bridge yelled at Sherm. "Em's my—"

He cut her off. "I wanted to. But I wasn't even sure you knew about it. I was trying not to tell *anyone!*"

Sherm looked at Em. "Look, I'm sorry. And I'm really sorry you have to tell your parents. But it's better than the picture going everywhere, isn't it? One kid had already posted it—never mind. Mr. Ramos made him take it down."

Em began to move. Slowly, she unzipped her backpack. And then she started whipping things at Sherm—pencil case, phone, binder.

He let the pencil case hit him, but he ducked the phone and the binder.

"Get out of here!" Em shrieked. "Just get out!"

Her voice seemed to hang in the air.

Sherm dropped his head and laced his fingers behind his neck. Then he looked up, as if he wanted to say something, glanced at Bridge, and left.

Em pulled up her knees again and rested her head on them. "I wish I were dead. Right now I sincerely wish I were dead."

"You don't mean that." Tab looked at Bridge, then up at the ceiling. "She doesn't mean it."

Em lifted her head and rolled her eyes. "It's an *expression*, Tab. Drama, much?"

"Say it," Tab said. "Say you don't mean it."

"Fine. I don't wish I were dead." Em actually smiled a little. "Geez, Tab." She leaned against Tab's shoulder. "Now I feel bad about Sherm," Em said.

They looked at Em's stuff, scattered across the tile floor.

"He was trying to help," Bridge said. She'd been thinking about it. "I'm not just sticking up for him." A big part of Bridge wanted to go find Sherm right now.

Em nodded, her head still on Tab's shoulder. "At least those idiots don't have my picture anymore. That's kind of good."

"Still," Tab said. "This is all so *unfair*. They're making it like you're the one who did something terrible. But it was Patrick. And David Marcel."

"I texted Patrick last night," Em said. "He swears he didn't send the picture to anyone. He says he didn't even *show* it to anyone. Someone grabbed his phone and started looking through his photos. That's who sent it around, as a joke or something."

"That's so pathetic," Tab said. "You don't believe him, do you?"

The bell rang, long and shrill. Longer and shriller than usual, it seemed to Bridge.

"You guys should go to class," Em said. "I'm staying right here."

But they didn't go. They stayed right there too.

CUPS

"Oh God," Em said to Bridge after last period. "My mom. You have to tell her with me. Or just—be there. You don't have to, but will you?"

"Of course I will. She won't even be mad, I bet. Your mom isn't the mad type."

Em was biting her nails. "Not mad. Upset."

She was right. After Em got her story out in one long rush, her mother moved closer to Em on the edge of the couch. "Why didn't you talk to me first?"

Em turned and looked at her. "Because I knew how stupid it was, I guess?"

"But I didn't even know this was *happening*. Honey, I didn't even *realize* you felt this way. About *anyone*."

And then: "I feel so *stupid*. I know this kind of thing goes on, and I should've *talked* to you about it."

And then: "Of course it's the 'child of divorce.' That's what they'll be thinking."

Em rolled her eyes. "Really, Mom? I doubt it."

Em's mom looked at Bridge. "Sweetie, can you give us five minutes? Evan's doing his cards—I know he'd love a fresh victim."

163

"Oh! Sure. Yeah." Bridge felt her face get hot. Should she have known to leave the room? Were they both wondering why she'd sat there watching? But Em had asked her to come.

Em glanced up and said, "Sorry, Bridge. I—"

"No, it's fine!" Bridge stood up quickly.

Em's little brother, Evan, sat in his room, his tarot cards spread out in front of him on his old play table. When Bridge walked in, he looked up as if he'd been expecting her.

"Oh good!" he said. "Can you sit?"

"Sure." Bridge took the small chair opposite his. "Haircut?" she asked. Evan's hair was extremely short, making his big-cheeked, nine-year-old face look even rounder than usual.

Evan gathered his cards into a pile. "Yeah. The guy went overboard, Mom says, but in a couple of weeks it'll look okay."

"It's nice. It—makes your eyelashes look long." She reached out to run her hand over the bristly top of his head.

He ducked her, jumped up, and went to his bed, where he grabbed a small navy-blue blanket that was jumbled up with his stuffed animals. He shook the blanket open over the table, letting it float down like a tablecloth. "This makes it more official," he told Bridge.

Then he sat down and laid out three cards, facedown, on the blanket. These three cards, he explained, represented her past, her present, and her future.

"I like to do present first," he said, flipping over the middle card. "Oh, I love cups! See the guy crossing the water?" He tapped the picture with one finger. "That means change is coming."

Evan said that this card, the eight of cups, meant she was "crossing over," leaving something behind and moving toward something she wanted.

"Okay, but isn't that kind of *everyone's* present?" Bridge said. "Leaving something behind? Moving toward something new?"

"But see how the guy is walking away all alone?" Evan said. "It's like he's kind of sad. So it might be more like an *inner* journey."

Bridge laughed.

Evan gave her a cloudy look. "It isn't a joke. And we can't really understand this card until we look at the past and the future. You have to look at them together. Okay, now let's do the past."

He flipped another card.

"Yikes," Bridge said. The picture on this one was grim: a man was lying facedown on the ground with a bunch of swords sticking out of his back.

"Ten of swords." Evan looked at it for a few seconds, almost glaring. "That doesn't really— Oh! It's from when you ran in front of the car!" He sounded pleased. "Now it makes sense."

Evan brought up Bridge's accident almost every time she saw him.

"I didn't *run* in front of—"

He tapped the card, all confidence again. "According to this, you're letting it hold you. Like hold you back." He crossed his short arms over his chest, demonstrating.

"I am not." But Bridge shivered. This was suddenly weird.

"Well, that's what you're crossing *away* from."

She forced another laugh. "On my 'inner journey,' you mean?"

"Let's do future," Evan said.

Em stuck her head in. "All done," she said. "Mom and Em: best friends again!" She gave Bridge a funny smile.

"We're not finished," Evan said. "You can watch, but not if you're going to talk."

Bridge thought Emily would come back with something snotty, but she just nodded, dragged a third little chair from next to Evan's bookshelf, and sat down, her knees bumping the table.

Even turned the last card. "Ace of cups!" He hit the table with two fists. "Okay, this is good. It means new beginnings— like a seed has been planted, kind of, but you might not know it yet."

"What seed?"

Evan shrugged. "Could be anything." He gathered his cards. "But whatever you're walking toward, it's kind of already there. Waiting."

Em was grinning. "Cups is the suit of *love*, Bridge."

Evan nodded. "Em got cups too, last time." He turned to her. "But remember, it was the two. That means shaky ground."

"Yeah, you told me. Thanks, Evan." Em stood up and pulled Bridge to her feet.

"Thanks, Evan," Bridge said. "That was great. Do I owe you anything?"

"Nah. Mom says I'm not allowed to charge money."

Bridge stopped in the doorway. "Evan," she said. "What if it had been the other way around? Cups in the past and swords in the future?"

"Oh, I would have figured out a way to make it sound good," Evan said, already shuffling again. "That's Mom's other rule."

Bridge and Emily were in the living room with Em's mom, eating peanut butter crackers and watching TV, when the doorbell rang.

Em's mom looked at her watch. "The sitter's early! And I wanted us to have a little snuggle time, especially today"— she looked quickly at Em—"I didn't mean that. It's a perfectly *normal* day. I mean, *you're* perfectly normal, sweetheart."

Em rolled her eyes. "Mom. Calm down."

"Do you want me to cancel dinner with Dad? I can cancel."

"No, you guys should do your divorce date," Em said. "But don't tell Dad everything, okay? Can't it wait a little?"

Em's mom considered. "I think I have to tell him, sweetie. You understand, right? Parents are partners."

Em flopped into the couch pillows. "I *knew* you'd say something like that."

"Sweetie—" Her mom stood up to answer the door.

Celeste stood there in a wet coat, taking her earbuds out. "Hey, guys. Hey, Em." She gave an awkward little wave. It was clear she'd been told the whole story.

Emily turned to her mom. "Can I go to Bridge's for dinner?" Her mom nodded.

THAT MUSIC

They walked to Bridge's in the rain.

"Your poor ears," Em said. She reached up to touch one as they crossed a street. "All wet and droopy." A turning car honked long and loud, then cut in front of them, wheels squeaking.

"Jerk!" Em yelled after it. "Can you believe that jerk?" she said, turning to Bridge.

Bridge was frozen. She wasn't hurt, but she couldn't move.

"Are you okay?" Em said. "Is it that thing again? When you get scared?"

"I'm okay," Bridge said. "Just give me a minute." She told her legs to get moving.

Em stood and stroked her hand.

Two teenage girls with a black umbrella and matching red purses ran past them in the rain. One of them turned around to shout at Bridge and Em. "Freaks!"

Em started laughing. And Bridge felt her legs come back.

"Now your ears are *really* wet," Em said when they were moving again. "Do you ever put them in the dryer?"

"I think they're dry-clean only," Bridge said.

"Sorry I laughed," Em said. "It was such a random moment. That stupid car, petting your arm in the rain, those stupid girls, and—this whole *day*."

"Actually," Bridge said, "the laughing helped."

When Bridge unlocked her apartment door and flung it open, the first thing she saw was Jamie, crawling down the hallway toward the kitchen.

Emily's hands flew to her mouth. "Oh no—what happened?"

"Don't worry," Bridge said quickly. "He's fine. He's just saving steps."

"Saving them for what?"

"For later. It's a bet."

"Another one?" Em whispered.

Jamie looked over his shoulder and gave them a little smile. "Yay, you're home. Can you grab me a banana? My knees are like little knobs of pain." He took a left and crawled toward the living room couch.

Bridge stepped out of her damp shoes, got a banana from the kitchen counter, walked to the couch, and dangled it in front of his face. "One dollar," she said.

"Can I owe you?"

"I guess, but I'm writing it down. Is Mom home?"

Jamie took the banana. "Do you think I'd pay you a dollar to get me a banana if Mom were here to do it for free?" He felt underneath the couch and came up with a book, which he started to read.

Bridge turned to Emily. "What do you feel like doing?"

Emily shrugged. "I don't know. Maybe just watch TV?"

"Any chance you guys could take this somewhere else?" Jamie pointed to his book. "Studying here."

"Jamie! This is the living room, not your private domain."

"I know. But I'm low on juice."

Bridge rolled her eyes. "Let's go to my room."

"So," Bridge said, landing cross-legged on her bed. "How're you doing?" She patted the space next to her.

"At this moment?" Em sat on the edge of the bed. "I don't even know. Did I tell you Patrick called my cell at one-thirty in the morning? He said after I texted him about the whole David Marcel thing, he felt so bad he couldn't sleep."

"But, Em, how did David Marcel get the picture in the first place?"

"I told you. Patrick says someone grabbed his phone."

"Who?"

"I don't know."

Em picked at the bedspread. "Did you know he's joining Banana Splits? We talked on the phone for almost an hour. Turns out his parents broke up last year too. Weird, right?"

"Wait. You don't hate him? At all?"

"I knew you'd say that. Now I'm double pathetic, right? He ruins my life and I'm still crushing on him."

Bridge was quiet.

"This is where you're supposed to tell me my life isn't ruined."

"Oh, sorry! Your life—"

"Kidding," Em said. "You know what? I actually like Patrick more now, in a way. He's like—a *person* now. His parents' divorce was way worse than mine. You should hear the things they say about each other. When I told him how mine are really good friends and still go out to dinner and stuff, he didn't believe me."

"So are you going to keep kissing him?"

Em laughed. "Well, not over the phone! Duh." She stretched out on the bed. "I don't know. We only kissed a few times. And last night was the first time we really talked, you know?"

It was still a little unreal that Em had kissed anyone. It was as if she'd been to the moon. But here she was, still Em.

Bridge bounced off the bed and sat in her desk chair, hunching forward to face Emily. "Em, I don't trust him. If he didn't send your picture to David, who did?"

"I told you, someone grabbed his phone! I know it sounds stupid, but I believe him. I just do." Emily gave her a big smile. "Things are different now. It's like the whole picture thing happened to two other people."

"*Two* other people? Emily, it happened to *you*. Not to him. He doesn't have to walk around knowing that half the school has seen—"

"But I don't mind," Em said quickly. "I mean, I do and I don't."

Bridge stared. "What are you talking about? You've been crying for two days."

"Yeah." Now Em started picking at the cuticle on her thumb. "But—don't think I'm stupid or anything, but I still like that picture. I never showed you which one I picked—it's the one where I'm looking to the side? And I used a filter— you can't see much, really. But I look good. Like you said."

"Are you saying you're *happy* this happened?"

171

Em picked her head up. "Are you insane? I'm just saying that I still like the picture. Noelle Park posted about ten pictures of herself in the Bahamas last Christmas. That little bikini, and no one said anything but how amazing she looked! What's wrong with looking amazing? I'm not ashamed of it."

Bridge chose her words carefully. "So why did you care? When Patrick—or whoever, this mystery person—sent the picture around? If you like it?"

Em shook her head. "Well, it was supposed to be just for him, you know? That's one thing. But the bad part wasn't that everyone was looking at the picture. I mean, it was weird and not great. But the bad part was that it felt like they were making fun of my feeling good about the picture. Of me *liking* myself. Does that even make sense?"

Bridge wanted to kill Patrick and David Marcel. Or at least utterly and completely humiliate them.

"You're not saying anything," Em said.

"I'm just getting angry," Bridge said. "All over again."

"Don't bother. Let's talk about something else." Em snapped her fingers and made an I've-got-a-great-idea face. "I know! You and Sherm."

"Are friends," Bridge said.

Em smiled. "More than friends, maybe?"

"Did you hear music?" Bridge asked, swiveling to face Em. "When you kissed Patrick?"

"Music," Em repeated.

"Yeah, my mom says that love is like music. One day you just—hear it."

"Whoa. First of all, I never said I loved Patrick. But I

think I know what she means. I don't think she means actual music, Bridge. She means that you know it when you feel it. Like music—you know it when you hear it."

"Okay, so love is also like a hamburger? You know it when you taste it?"

Em laughed. "A hamburger is more deliberate. You have to make it, or ask for it. . . . Music just kind of breaks over you."

"She also says hearing the music is different from wanting to dance. And knowing who you want to dance with—that's different from hearing the music."

Em flopped back on the bed and laughed into Bridge's pillow.

"What?" Bridge said. *"What?"*

"Nothing," Em said. "I just love your mom."

"Yeah, she's a nut."

"But you like Sherm, don't you, Bridge? It's kind of obvious."

Was it obvious? Bridge thought about the way she looked for him at school now. The cafeteria used to just be the cafeteria. Now it was the cafeteria *and Sherm might be in it.* And English wasn't English anymore. Now English was *definitely seeing Sherm.* But she didn't want to meet him behind the science lab.

"How did you know you liked Patrick?"

Em smiled. "How did I know? I think about him all the time."

"But you guys don't spend any time together. Maybe what you like is some fake idea of who he is."

"I just told you, it's different now. We talk to each other."

"Once. You talked once."

"For an hour! And stop changing the subject." Em sat up and crossed her legs. "Tell me two things you know about Sherm. Two things you know *for sure*."

"He's nice."

Em shook her head. "Lame. Two real things."

"Fine. One: he smells a little like bread."

At least, his shirt smelled like bread. What did that mean? That she'd smelled his shirt?

"Okay," Em said. "What else?"

"He misses his grandfather, who used to live with him."

"Aw, his grandpa died?"

"No. He left Sherm's grandmother. Moved out over the summer."

"Really? Wow. The curse of the nine thousand things."

"I guess."

"Anyway," Em said. "You like Sherm. Definitely."

"How do you know?"

"I just know."

"I don't want to kiss him or anything," Bridge said quickly.

"No?"

Bridge shook her head.

"Hmm," Em said. "You know what?"

"What?"

"I think you just need more time. Put a pin in it."

Bridge wondered if you ever found your dance partner *before* you heard the music.

• • •

That night, Bridge woke with a shudder and a frantic intake of air. Rising from the dark of the mummy dream, she threw her arms wide, drew her knees up, and kicked her covers half-way down the bed. Not far enough. She kicked and kicked until everything was on the floor.

"I'm here," her mother said quietly. She stood near but knew not to try to hug Bridge or touch her right away. What Bridge needed was space. Once the dream receded—the feeling of paralysis, the suffocating closeness of it—her body relaxed, and her mom came closer.

"You're okay," her mom said, brushing Bridge's hair back from her forehead and letting her fingers run lightly along Bridge's scalp. It was something she'd started doing when Bridge was in the hospital, because the rest of Bridge's body was in some sort of cast or sling. "You're okay," her mom said again, soothingly.

But Bridge was already asleep.

SHERM

December 2

Dear Nonno Gio,

    I'm pretty sure she hates me now. And most of the guys are mad too. They all know I told Mr. Ramos about the picture going around. But Patrick actually texted me to say what I did was cool. He said he didn't have the guts! Which just goes to show.

    Actually I have no idea what it goes to show.

Sherm

P.S. Two months and twelve days till your birthday.

VALENTINE'S DAY

Gina lives only a mile from your high school, and sometimes she walks. Back in the fall, when you were first getting to know her, you saw her coming down the block with Marco Saks, talking.

"You know Marco Saks?" you asked Gina.

She nodded. "Oh yeah—since we were two. Our families rent a house together every summer for a month. We kind of grew up together."

"You grew up with Marco Saks? The sophomore lusted after by ninety percent of the girls at school?" Or whatever percentage of them had decent vision and a male-oriented libido. Because Marco Saks is beautiful. There's no other word for what Marco Saks is.

She smiled. "I know. Everyone's in love with him. But he's an only child, like me, and now he's like my big brother. Actually, I like to call him my *little* brother." She laughed. "It annoys the hell out of him."

Gina is tall.

It wasn't even a month later that, in her bedroom, Gina whispered, "Can I trust you? Because I can't hold this in anymore and I think you're the nicest person I've met in at least five years. I think I can trust you. Am I right?"

No one had ever talked to you like that before, but you don't dwell on it now—you don't think about how good it made you feel to have another person say "I like you. I trust you." None of Vinny's games.

"Of course you can trust me," you said.

"I can, right?" She looked into your eyes, her color rising fast behind the dark freckles that sprinkled her nose and cheeks, even in October. Then she said, "I'm in love with him."

You didn't get it. "Who?"

She covered her face with her hands and whispered into them. "Marco."

"Whoa. Really? But you said he's like—"

She nodded. "We were babies together! His parents are my *godparents*."

"Does he know how you feel?"

"No! He has no idea. And I can't tell him—it would wreck everything. I don't even understand how it happened. But it's been almost two years."

"Two *years?*"

"Yes!" Gina smiled. "Two years. And it feels so good to have someone I can tell. Most of the girls at my middle school were such bitches."

A vaguely familiar kid with sunglasses and a smirk on his face is hovering near the cash register. Adrienne looks up and groans. "Not again."

"Hey, beautiful."

"Don't call me beautiful, kid."

"I'm sixteen."

"Sixteen going on twelve."

His confidence is unshaken. "Can I get a smoothie?"

You remember now: he's Alex, from middle school. He was a year ahead of you, and you're pretty sure he's still a friend of Bridge's brother.

Adrienne puts a hand on her hip. "What kind of smoothie?"

He smiles. "You pick something out for me."

She pats her shoulders. "Me pick?"

Alex nods.

Adrienne turns her back on him and walks over to the smoothie blender. You watch Alex read the back of her T-shirt. He shakes his head, smiling as if she's adorable. He's so arrogant. You never understood why Jamie liked him.

Then you catch yourself having that thought and laugh.

"Hey," Alex says, noticing you.

"Hey," you say back.

"I forget your name," he says.

"That's okay," you tell him. "Is school out already?"

He gives you a funny look. "No, I have a free period."

Adrienne comes back, holding what looks like a glass of frothy milk with brown and green stuff floating in it.

"That's—a smoothie?" Alex says.

She nods. "You told me to pick the ingredients."

"Is this because of the other night with Jamie?"

"Don't you want to know what's in it?"

"Okay. What's in it?"

"Milk. And I threw a whole-wheat spinach-feta wrap in there." She holds it out. "It's healthy! Five fifty, please."

"You're kidding, right?"

She glares. "You asked me to pick the ingredients. Did you or didn't you?"

He pays.

When he's gone, Adrienne looks at you. "Annoying guy," she says.

"What did he mean? When he said 'Is this because of the other night with Jamie?'"

"Not much of a story," she says. "Jamie is kind of sweet. But he needs to find some new friends."

"Yeah."

Adrienne picks at what's left of her banana-chocolate-chip muffin. "Whatever it is that's bugging you," she says, "it's about a guy, right?"

"No. It's not about a guy. And nothing happened to me."

"Something happened to you," she says. "Or some*one* happened to you."

No, you think. I happened to someone.

COOL

Bridge was four blocks from school when she saw Sherm standing on the corner ahead of her. Just standing there.

"Hey," she said when she reached him.

"Hey," Sherm said. "I saw you coming, so I waited."

"Thanks."

After two blocks of what Jamie would definitely call awkward silence, Bridge said, "Em isn't mad, you know. She's sorry she threw that stuff at you. She feels bad."

Sherm nodded. "What about you? Are you still mad?"

"Me? *I'm* not mad. I was upset for a second that you didn't tell me you were going to tell Mr. Ramos. But I get it. You didn't know for sure that I even knew about the picture."

This would have been a good time to say that she had actually helped Em take the picture. But she didn't want to admit that to Sherm, or even think about it.

"Remember your riddle?" Sherm said. "The two brothers and the two doors?"

"Yeah."

"I had to pick a door. You know? If I hadn't said anything, that picture would be everywhere by now."

"I can't believe Patrick didn't get suspended," Bridge said.

"He says he didn't send it."

"I know. Someone 'grabbed his phone.'"

"And sent it to David Marcel," Sherm finished.

"David Marcel got it first?"

"Yeah, and he sent it to at least ten guys right away."

"Seriously? Why didn't *he* get suspended?"

Sherm looked surprised. "He did get suspended. You didn't know?"

"No. You're sure?"

"Oh, I'm sure. I'm sure David Marcel got suspended because he hates me now. And so do a lot of his friends."

Sherm had made a sacrifice, really. And then Emily had thrown half her stuff at his head. Poor Sherm. "Wow," Bridge told him. "You were looking at two crummy doors."

He laughed. "Yeah. But I just picked the one David Marcel wasn't standing in front of. Not that hard."

When they got to school, Sherm said, "So, tomorrow morning, same corner?"

Bridge hadn't expected that. "Okay. What time?"

"Eight?"

"Sure."

"Cool."

LITTLE BY LITTLE

Bridge watched as her mom tried to zip her suitcase. She got stuck on a boot heel at the third corner, unzipped the bag, and laid it open on the floor to rearrange her things.

"It's only three days," she told Bridge, "but you wouldn't believe the number of events—we're playing at the rehearsal dinner, the prewedding cocktail hour, the ceremony, and then—get this—there's a *high tea* the day after."

Her first fancy wedding had been a big success, and now she was getting other jobs. This one was a last-minute fill-in for a famous violinist who'd gone down with the flu.

"What's high tea?" Bridge asked.

"Oh, just a big spread, I think—lots of little sandwiches and pastries. And, you know, tea."

"Yum."

"Yeah, yum. Though I'll have my hands full." Bridge's mom tilted her head toward the cello case leaning against the closet mirror.

She knelt and tried to zip the bag again. It still wouldn't close. She yanked out one of the boots. "Looks like I'll have to wear these on the plane."

Bridge smiled.

"Sweetie," her mom said, feeling for the other boot, "we need to talk."

Em had warned Bridge. "The moms have been talking," she said in homeroom. "This is definitely going to come up at home. Feel free to express your shock and disgust at my behavior."

"About the thing with Em, you mean?" Bridge said. "Don't worry. I'm not going to do anything like that."

"I just wish she'd talked to her parents about what was going on. You would talk to me, right, Bridge? You'd tell me if you felt that way about someone? If you were thinking of doing something like that?"

"Sure. I'd tell you."

Her mom stood up. "So . . . *is* there anything you want to tell me? About anyone, I mean?"

Bridge looked back at her. "Nope."

"Great." Her mom smiled. "I mean—"

"Don't worry, I know what you meant."

"Great." Bridge saw her mom mentally checking this task off of her to-do list. Then she said, "Is Em okay?"

"She's okay, yeah."

Her mom started pulling on a boot. "When I was your age, I went with my friend Marjorie to get my ears pierced—without permission."

"You did?"

"Yes. But when I got home, Grandma told me that I was under the mistaken impression that my body belonged to me. She said that until I turned eighteen, it actually belonged to her. And she hadn't given anyone permission to put holes in it."

184

"Seriously?"

Stepping into the second boot, Bridge's mom nodded. "She was *very* serious. She made me take the earrings out and let the holes close up." She stood up, stamped once to make her dress fall straight, and looked at herself in the mirror. "You think the boots work with this?"

"Definitely."

Her mom caught Bridge's eyes in the mirror. "Grandma was wrong, Bridge. She was wrong. My body was mine. Your body is yours."

"Okay."

"Especially *your* body, Bridge. You earned it back, little by little. Don't forget that."

Then she zipped her suitcase closed.

SHERM

December 10

Dear Nonno Gio,

Last night Dad and I were at the table, just us.

He said, "How are you doing, hon?" And I honestly
didn't know what I was supposed to tell him. I said, "Good.
You?" and Dad said, "You know what? I think this whole
time I've been convinced that Nonno's coming back. It just
seems like a joke, doesn't it? Or something? And I've been
waiting."

And I said, "Yeah."

Dad told me that you called him at work, to give him your
new address in Hoboken. That you asked about me. You told
him you'd been trying my cell.

Well, I saw your voice mails and deleted them. Dad didn't
know.

Dad says you still love us. He's like the perfect poster child
for divorce:

Adults are complicated!

Sometimes people change!

But everyone still loves the kids so much!

I nodded at him like I was supposed to. But you <u>moved</u> <u>out</u>. That and your supposed love are two supermagnets that repel each other. No matter how hard I try, I can't make them touch.

Sherm

P.S. Two months, four days.

NOT LITERALLY

Just before winter vacation, Bridge watched as the letters from the Talentine committee were distributed in homeroom. Emily slid hers into her binder without opening it. Then she turned and smiled at Bridge. It was such a careful smile. Bridge got a terrible feeling.

"Can you believe this? I got dinged!" Em waved her letter in the hall after class. "And I know why."

"There were so many good singers," Tab said. "You picked the hardest thing to go for. They said singing was the most competitive—"

"Oh please. That's not why! It's because of you-know-what. This stupid school hates me."

"Nobody hates you," Bridge said. "Em, they said there aren't that many spots for seventh graders, remember? You guys will get in next year."

Tab shrugged her knapsack down from her shoulder so that it dangled from her elbow. "I got in, actually—but it was only because I was, like, the only juggler."

Em stared at Tab for a second and then said, "You know what? I'm turning into a huge jerk. I didn't even ask whether you got in. But—this is amazing. Now Bridge and I have a reason to go to the show. We'll sit in the front row and cheer for you."

"Actually," Bridge said, "I have to do Tech Crew stuff—we kind of design the whole show, and then we run the lights and sound and everything."

"That's so cool!" Tab said. "I went to the show back when Celeste was in it, and they did this crazy psychedelic ghost-town cowboy theme: rainbows, tumbleweeds, and a gigantic papier-mâché . . . um, I think it was a horse, but it might have been a unicorn."

Bridge made a face. "I hope we come up with something better than that."

"No, it was cool."

Em looked at them. "Well, then I'll sit by myself and cheer you both on. And we'll meet up after. Okay? It's a plan!" She marched off toward class.

Tab and Bridge watched her go. "Those jerks," Tab said.

"Who?" Bridge asked.

Tab spun to look at Bridge. "Don't you get it? They totally banned her. You were there. Her audition was crazy good! Definitely one of the best."

"So why didn't you say so? To Emily?"

"I thought it would make her feel even worse. This makes me want to kill someone!"

"You? Kill someone?"

Tab sighed. "Well, not literally. Come on. We have French."

VALENTINE'S DAY

Why you're there, at the Bean Bar, wrapping day-old muffins, has nothing to do with a boy. Not exactly.

It started right before Halloween, at Dollar-Eight. The four of you were at the big round booth in the back.

"Let's play truth or dare!" Zoe said. Truth or dare always gets an automatic yes from Vinny.

"Okay," Vinny said, leaning forward. "I'll start. Something really easy." She pointed at Gina. "Who's your crush?"

"My crush?" Gina looked sick. She has one of those faces that can't hide anything.

"You're supposed to ask her truth or dare," you said. "You didn't even ask what she wanted."

Vinny ignored you. "Crush. Spill it. Here and now." She knocked on the table, gave Gina a friendly smile.

Gina shook her head. "It's complicated."

Vinny's smile changed. "Complicated?" Your head began to ping. You knew that smile. You tried to send Gina a telepathic message: *Just make something up.*

But Gina isn't like that. She smiled back shyly. "Yeah. It's not that I don't *want* to tell you. I just literally *can't*. Can I tell you something else? A different truth?"

Vinny straightened her back, and you saw Zoe do the same. Did she even know how precisely she copied everything Vinny did?

"That's not how it works," Vinny said, sounding genuinely sympathetic. Vinny was truly genius at being awful while looking incredibly nice. Part of you had to stand back and almost admire it. "If you refuse to tell the truth," she said, "you have to do a dare."

"Oh—right." Gina looked relieved. "Great. I'll do the dare."

"So you'll definitely do the dare?"

"Sure."

Vinny tossed her a ChapStick and said, "Okay. Here you go."

Gina caught it, smiled. "What do I do with this?"

"Eat it. Obviously."

Gina's smile caved in. "You're not serious."

"It's not poisonous or anything," Vinny said reassuringly. "I know someone who ate one, and she was fine."

"Voluntarily?" Gina asked. Her eyes went to you, then dropped to the ChapStick in her hand.

Vinny was lying. Either that or she had once made poor Zoe eat a ChapStick.

"Look, are you playing or not?" Vinny said. "You can leave any time you want."

Gina's face. She looked at you again.

"Really? Eating ChapStick?" you asked Vinny. "Did you think of that yourself?"

"She wouldn't do the truth," Vinny said. "She gets the dare."

"Okay, but what you're asking her to do is actually"—you deliberately dropped your voice—"*disgusting.*"

Disgusting was, to Vinny, the lowest of the low. The idea that she herself might be disgusting had clearly never entered her mind.

"Excuse me?"

"Think about it," you say. "It's kind of a disgusting idea." You turned to Zoe. "Did you come up with it?"

"No!" Zoe squealed, and then looked guiltily at Vinny.

Vinny stood up. "Game over," she said, and walked away. After a pause, Zoe jumped up and scrambled after her, snatching her purse from the back of her chair—it was dark red, just like Vinny's.

"Wow," Gina said when they were gone. She smiled, but her face was sad all over. "She hates me a lot, huh?"

"She'll get over it," you said.

"It's because we're friends," Gina said. "You and me."

"Vinny has a lot of friends," you tell her.

"Yeah." Gina opened the ChapStick and used it on her lips. "But we're the kind who would never hurt each other."

The next day, Vinny and Zoe looked right through you. After lunch, you found a little pink envelope in your locker with your name on it. Inside was one of those invitations for a little-kid party, with a cute parade of animals in party hats on the front. You opened it and saw it was the preprinted kind, with "You Are Invited" at the top and blank lines underneath where you're supposed to write

192

in the details. Someone had filled them in with a black marker:

Un
You Are ^Invited!
What: Vinny's Halloween Bash
Where: Zoe's place
When: Halloween. Duh.
Why: Think about it.
Glad you won't be there!

Uninvited. If "umpteen" is the best word in the world, maybe "uninvited" is the worst. It shouldn't even be a word. It shouldn't be anything.

TECH CREW

The full tech crew had been called for a Wednesday meeting, and they were all squeezed together backstage. Bridge was close enough to smell Sherm's bread smell. Mr. Partridge had ordered pizza again. Now he stood in front of a whiteboard he'd propped up against an old piece of scenery. From her spot on the floor, Bridge could make out some blue sky and the back end of a large pink pig.

Mr. Partridge glanced at his watch. "Quickly, people. We don't have much more time." He tapped the board, where he'd written their list of Talentine show themes in purple block letters:

ITALIAN RESTAURANT
NORTH POLE (PENGUINS)
APOLLO 11 MOON LANDING
ROMAN BATH
THE SIXTIES/HIPPIES
RAIN FOREST

"I don't think there are penguins at the North Pole," Bridge whispered to Sherm. "They're all in Antarctica."

"Good point," Sherm said. "Why'd you nominate the moon landing?"

"Because. I thought we could try it out."

He gave her a questioning look.

"A fake moon landing," she said. "We'll make one of those landing-pod things, and we'll get a flag, and—I don't know, rocks? Come on, just vote for it."

The sixties was a strong contender. "Four votes!" Mr. Partridge said, making a note on the board. "There may be some tie-dyeing in our future. Okay, who's for the moon landing?"

Hands went up. Sherm hesitated. One arm waving wildly, Bridge reached out with the other, grabbed Sherm's wrist, and held it up.

Mr. Partridge smiled. "Bridge, please release Sherman."

Everyone laughed. She let go.

Sherm's arm dropped, but a second later he put it up again.

"Okay, folks, we have a winner." Mr. Partridge drew a circle around the words "Apollo 11." "We're going to the moon."

A few kids cheered. Bridge did a mini-fist-pump.

"Remember," Mr. Partridge said. "This is a secret. Anyone who spills the beans has to pay double for their T-shirt. Understood?"

When the meeting was over, Bridge waited for Mr. Partridge by the auditorium doors.

"Question, Bridge?" He was still coming up the aisle toward her. It occurred to Bridge that Mr. Partridge was on the older side.

"You were a judge, right? For the auditions?"

"Yes."

"Why didn't Emily make it? I was there. She was one of the best."

Mr. Partridge stopped. "Let me ask you a couple of questions. How many judges were there?" he asked.

"Three."

"And how many people am I?"

"One."

"Exactly."

Bridge only hesitated for a second. "So she *was* banned?"

He shook his head. "Nothing that formal. But unofficially, yes."

"But that's completely unfair!"

"And," he said, looking at her, "it's exactly how most unfair things happen."

"Did you even say anything? Fight for her?"

He blinked. "Bridget, I know how to pick my battles. This conversation is over."

Bridge and her parents were on the couch, watching the annual network broadcast of *Rudolph the Red-Nosed Reindeer*, when they heard the front door slam and the now-familiar sound of Jamie's enormous steps.

"How was practice?" Bridge's mom called.

"Fine," Jamie called back.

"It's Rudolph!" Bridge yelled. "Hurry up! We're almost up to Hermey's big moment."

"No thanks." And his door closed.

Bridge looked at her parents. "Did he just say 'No thanks'?"

They told her to give him a few minutes alone. Her mom handed her a candy cane.

After the movie, Bridge knocked on Jamie's door. "You wrecked Rudolph night!" she yelled. Without waiting, she opened the door. "Rudolph is no fun without you."

"Sure, come right in," Jamie said. "That's what I meant to say when I closed my door."

He was still in his track clothes, lying on the bed with his computer resting on his chest. On the floor next to the bed was an empty bowl stained with red sauce.

"You ate *all* the meatballs?" Bridge said.

"Running makes me hungry," Jamie said. He swiveled his laptop around to face her and said, "Check this out."

Bridge leaned forward. It was an eBay listing for a Rolling Stones T-shirt: the 1981 North American Tour. The same shirt he'd lost to Alex almost a year ago. "A hundred dollars? Wow."

"Yeah. Can you believe I bought it for seven bucks? When's that gonna happen again?"

"You know Grandma and Grandpa would buy you another one. For Christmas. Or Mom and Dad—they have all that celebrity-wedding money coming in."

Their mom's second fancy wedding had been a bigger hit than her first. She'd just booked two more jobs.

Jamie shook his head. "No way. I told you, I'm winning it back." He shut the laptop. "Only a loser would pay a hundred bucks for a T-shirt. It's not even cool anymore if you pay that much for it."

Bridge took Hermey the elf from Jamie's bookshelf. "So what are you going to ask for? For Christmas?"

"Maybe a new best friend."

"That's a good idea."

"Get me an ice cream sandwich from the freezer?" Jamie asked. "I barely have enough juice left to go brush my teeth."

"Sure. For two bucks."

He grinned. "How about a nickel?"

"Fifty cents," she said. "I'm saving for my Tech Crew T-shirt. I need to have it in time for the Talentine show."

"A quarter?" Jamie countered.

Bridge felt kind of sorry for him. She tossed him Hermey and said, "It's a deal."

Bridge was sleeping that night when a door slammed, waking her up. She looked at her clock: 12:01.

A minute later, she heard the bathroom door open, steps coming down the hall, and then Jamie's door, closing quietly.

"Hey, was that you slamming doors in the middle of the night?" she asked him in the kitchen the next morning.

"Sorry." He looked embarrassed. "I was waiting for midnight. I closed the bathroom door too hard."

"Waiting for midnight?"

"Yeah. I always get into bed on step ten thousand, right? So then if, you know, *nature calls*, I have to wait until it's officially the next day."

"Jamie," Bridge said, shaking a cereal box to see how much was left. "You really do need a new best friend."

SLEEVES

On the first day back after every vacation, school lunch came with a cupcake, so Bridge left her bag lunch at home. From across the cafeteria, she spotted Em walking toward their corner table, wearing a baggy green sweatshirt and carrying her tray. Tab wasn't coming; the Human Rights Club met on Tuesdays at lunch, and even a cupcake couldn't persuade her to miss quality time with the Berperson.

"Aren't you hot in that thing?" Bridge asked, catching up to Emily. "I feel like we're in a furnace." It was always like that, once the school turned on the heat.

"Yeah," Em started, "I'm—" and then she burst into tears. She just stood there with her tray and let them come.

"Hold on." Bridge held her tray in one hand and took Em's with the other. She slid both trays—sandwich, milk, cupcake—onto the table, and then she grabbed Em's hand and led her out of the cafeteria.

In the bathroom, Em was nearly choking on tears and snot. "They said . . . I have to wear this stupid sweatshirt. It's from the lost and found. They said"—she wiped her face with a fist—"my shirt was too revealing!"

"Revealing?" Bridge ducked into a stall and came out with some balled-up toilet paper.

"Spaghetti straps!" Emily sobbed out the words.

"What?" Bridge said. "Breathe, okay? I can't understand you. It sounded like you said 'spaghetti.'"

Em shook her head. "Spaghetti straps. They aren't *sleeves*, they said."

"Oh."

Em took a breath, calmed down. "You can wear cat ears all day, but I can't wear my own shirt."

"Hey!"

"Sorry." Em blew her nose, folded the toilet paper, and wiped her eyes. "I'm sorry. That was jerky."

"It's okay," Bridge said. "I get it."

Em sniffed, exhaled.

"Tab and I agree with you, you know. About the Talentine show. It's not fair."

"Yeah, well, whatever. I'm not really in the mood to sing anyway."

"Because of this?" Bridge pointed to the sweatshirt.

"Did you know that David Marcel calls me a skank every time he sees me?"

"He *what?*"

"Yeah. So I get to hear that at least six times a day."

"Emily, tell someone. Tell Mr. Ramos!"

"Sure, my new friend Mr. Ramos."

"So tell Mr. P."

She shook her head. "Mr. P already went to bat for me. He's pretty much the reason I didn't get suspended for sending the picture to Patrick in the first place."

"He is?"

Em nodded. "That's what my mom says. Anyway, telling will just make things worse. Patrick says David Marcel is still pissed about getting suspended. And his parents took away his phone. Can you believe he hasn't had a phone since November?" She smiled the smallest of smiles.

"You're still talking to Patrick, huh?" Bridge tried to keep her face neutral.

Em's smile got bigger. "Of course. Still just friends. Did I tell you? He came to a Banana Splits meeting."

Bridge said nothing.

"He's a good guy, Bridge. Really."

"A good guy whose phone was grabbed by a mystery person who texted your picture to David Marcel, who sent it to half the class."

"I know you don't believe him. But Patrick says he never even *showed* that picture to David Marcel. He wouldn't."

"So why won't he tell you who *did*?"

"I don't know." Em closed her eyes and leaned her head back against the wall.

"Sorry," Bridge said. "I'll shut up."

Em opened one eye. "You don't want to go back for those cupcakes, do you? We could eat them in here if it doesn't gross you out."

When Bridge walked into first period the next morning, there was a sheet of paper face-up on every desk.

"A *quiz*?" someone whined.

But it wasn't a quiz. It was a copy of the school's dress code.

DRESS CODE/REGULATIONS FOR SCHOOL ATTIRE

The purpose of this dress code is to ensure that all students dress appropriately for school and school activities.

- Tank tops and shirts with spaghetti straps or other types of straps are prohibited.
- Shirts, pants, or skirts that reveal a bare midriff are prohibited.
- Miniskirts and short shorts are prohibited. <u>The hem of skirts and shorts must reach the knee.</u>
- Baggy pants must be worn at the waist.

"To the *knee?*" Tab said at lunch. "Who has shorts that go down to the knee? Wait till Celeste sees this. She'll die laughing."

"You know why they passed this out, right?" Emily asked. "It's because of me. Yesterday when they made me wear that gross sweatshirt from the lost and found? I told them I had never even heard of their stupid dress code."

"Did you really say 'stupid'? Good for you!" Tab said.

Em looked down at the table. "I wish I had."

"I didn't know about the dress code either," Bridge said.

"They said it's on the website," Em said. "I mean, who looks at the website?"

"Other kids wear spaghetti straps to school," Bridge said.

"The dress code isn't for them," Em said. "It's for people like me. Bad girls."

"Bad girls!" Tab erupted. "Emily. What are you talking about?"

"I think they wish I would just go away and not corrupt good girls like you."

"You didn't corrupt anyone," Tab said angrily. "Patrick wanted that picture. And what about the picture he sent you? They're acting like this was all your idea or something. It's such a double standard!"

Em shook her head. "You guys told me not to do it. I'm stupid." She took the sheet of paper from Tab's hand. "This isn't for you. It's for people like me." And she stomped away.

BINGO

Now that it was January, Tech Crew began to meet after school twice a week to get ready for the Talentine show. The landing capsule was still in the planning stages, but there was a lot of backdrop to be painted: midnight blue with silver stars and Earth glowing in the distance.

"This is going to be so cool," Bridge said, taking a smock from the pile in the middle of the stage floor.

"Agreed," Mr. Partridge said. "It'll be a nightmare to prime all of this when we have to repaint for the spring play, but for now it will be very cool."

Bridge didn't think it would be a nightmare to repaint everything for the spring play. In fact, she didn't believe that Tech Crew could ever be anything but fun.

Sherm had volunteered to bring in an American flag, and when Mr. Partridge asked if Sherm could "by any chance fetch it today," Bridge volunteered to go with him. She had never seen Sherm's house. The thought of walking there with him—and then back to school, where Mr. Partridge had promised everyone pizza later—filled her with a new kind of happiness.

"My grandfather has all these flags," Sherm told Bridge on the way to his house. "I think they're still in the closet."

"Your grandmother won't mind you taking one?"

"Nah."

Sherm lived in one of the brownstones that lined a few side streets on the west side of Broadway. Large steps led from the sidewalk to a front door. While Sherm unlocked it, Bridge noticed a little metal plate mounted above the doorbell:

Drs. Apollo and Eleanor Russo

"Apollo!" Bridge said, pointing. "That's your dad's name?"

"Yup."

"Like Apollo 11! That's so funny!"

"It's hilarious." Sherm shoved the door open with his hip, revealing a carpeted hallway and a broad wooden staircase.

Bridge inhaled. "Mmm. What is that *smell?*"

Sherm sniffed. "Cookies, I think." A smile spread across his face. "Welcome to *my* planet," he said.

"Planet cookie," Bridge said. "Lucky you."

"The flag's up here," Sherm said, starting up the stairs. Bridge followed.

At the top of the stairs was a little area with a fireplace and two small couches that faced each other. Sherm crossed it to a wooden door that stood open, revealing a bright room: a big bed, a desk, a tall dresser, and under the window, a trunk. "My grandmother's room," Sherm announced. "Everything in its place."

"I kind of love it," Bridge said, walking in. The desk was the nicest thing in it—glossy dark wood, thin straight legs. Bridge pointed at the two perfectly squared stacks of paper and the black-and-gold pen that lay between them. "She likes to write?"

"She's a translator—English to Italian."

"Wow." Bridge leaned to look and saw a page of slanted handwriting in perfect lines. "Is this—poetry or something?"

Sherm grinned. "I have no idea. I can't read it. But a lot of her jobs are junky self-help books that she complains about. She's more of a science fiction fan."

Bridge moved on, stopping in front of a few framed photos on the wall next to the window. She pointed to one: four dark-haired women with fishing poles.

"Is one of these your grandmother?"

"Yeah. The tall one."

There was nothing made-up about her, but she was almost movie-star beautiful. "Wow," Bridge said again.

Sherm smiled. "She says she was 'the prize of Gela.' That's a town in Sicily. And she still loves to go fishing." He glanced at Bridge. "I'll get the flag."

"The prize, huh?" Bridge briefly imagined what Tab would say about that. "You look like her, actually."

"I look like my grandfather," Sherm said quickly. Then he seemed embarrassed. "That's what people say." He pointed to a photo of three young men standing close, arms looped around shoulders.

Bridge looked. "The middle one?" Because one of them was unmistakably Sherm-like: nice-looking, with curly hair and—she didn't know what made people look like one another, she realized. The jawline? The one dimple? The chin?

Sherm was in the closet, pulling things off a shelf. "Yep, middle one."

"But you have your grandmother's eyes," Bridge said. His grandfather's were smaller.

"If you say so."

"Hey—a VW Bug!" She pointed to a picture of a smiling dark-haired couple in graduation caps holding hands in front of a yellow Volkswagen Beetle.

A moment of silence. "That was my mom's. She sold it a long time ago."

"Too bad," Bridge said.

Sherm held up a red-and-white bundle. "Bingo! One American flag."

Bridge laughed. "Bingo?"

Sherm's neck blushed. "Oh—my grandfather used to say that all the time." He shrugged. "Maybe it's being in his room. I mean, his old room. Let's go." Holding the flag under one arm, he crossed the room and slipped his hand into hers. The room disappeared.

They were holding hands.

She didn't know what to do. She didn't want to squeeze or to let her hand go limp, but everything she did felt like one or the other, and suddenly all she could think about was keeping her fingers lined up normally and applying exactly the right kind of pressure. She was sure that Sherm could tell she had no idea what she was doing.

"Maybe we can snag some cookies on the way out," he said, pretending nothing unusual was happening.

"Mm," Bridge said.

Still holding on, he led her down the stairs. He let go just before they got to the kitchen, which was a relief.

Sherm's grandmother was at the stove, with her back to them.

"Bye, Na!" Sherm came up behind her and kissed her cheek. "Oh, this is Bridge."

Sherm's grandmother turned, and Bridge could see the woman in the picture upstairs, along with a lot of years. She held Sherm's face in her two hands and kissed the air in front of him. Then she turned to Bridge and reached for her hand. Bridge gave her the other one—the one Sherm had not just been holding.

"Bridget. I'm so glad that you are here with us."

"Oh—thanks," Bridge said.

"It's Bridge, Na. Not Bridget."

His grandmother nodded. "You will both eat something now," she said.

Sherm said, "We can't—we're going back to school, to work on the show. I just came for the flag. Unless there are cookies?"

Sherm's grandmother looked at the flag. Then she walked to a little pantry off the kitchen and came back with a plate of small brown cookies. She thrust it at them. "As many as you want!"

They each took three.

"Thanks," Sherm said, kissing her goodbye.

"Take care of it," Sherm's grandmother said.

For a strange moment, Bridge thought that *she* was the "it." Then she realized: Sherm's grandmother meant the flag.

Walking back to school, Bridge and Sherm ate their cookies and didn't hold hands. "These are amazing," Bridge said.

And they were: buttery and almond-tasting, with a hint of lemon. Not at all what Bridge had expected.

At home later, Bridge stood at the living room windows, counting the blocks between her building and Sherm's house—two up, one over. Then she realized she could actually make out a corner of his roof in the dark.

She thought about Sherm holding her hand. She didn't think she wanted Sherm to like her like that. Because if she didn't like him back, could they still be friends?

If they couldn't be friends, she thought, her heart might break.

But wait. Did that mean she liked him?

She looked at Sherm's roof.

"It's getting dark so early these days."

Bridge whirled. Her mother stood behind her, squinting out the window.

"You're back! How was it?" It was getting hard to keep track of her mom's comings and goings. She was always packing and unpacking.

"It was great—but after this next one, I'm taking a break. I miss you guys. Where's Jamie?"

"I'm not sure—track practice?"

Her mom sighed. "Sometimes I miss the old days. When everyone was little and we all stayed at home together."

"Yeah," Bridge said. "Me too."

"But *you're* still little," her mom said, reaching for Bridge with her fingers wiggling. "Little enough to tickle!"

"Stop!" Bridge said. "Tickling is torture!" But she took a step toward her mother.

SHERM

January 16

Dear Nonno Gio,

I was in your room with Bridge today, and she looked at some of the pictures. (She says I look like you, big surprise.) We borrowed one of your flags for school, but I'll put it back in a few weeks. Maybe you don't even care about those flags anymore?

She kept saying how beautiful Nonna is. You used to say that too, all the time. Remember those last two weeks before you moved out? Everyone was upset and Nonna cried a lot and Dad was still trying to get you and her to take a trip back to Italy, like maybe that would remind you who you were. He got mad at you and yelled, "What do you mean, *why*? Because you've turned into a stranger!"

We pretend there's such a thing as a private conversation in this house, but I have always been able to hear everything from the hall outside my bedroom. I heard you tell Dad that you didn't expect him to understand. You said that, in a way, you were a stranger to yourself. It scared me.

But I almost understand. Sometimes I feel like a stranger

to myself too. Today I held Bridge's hand in your room. I saw her hand and the next thing I knew I was holding on to it. We both pretended nothing was happening.

I guess my question is: Is the <u>new</u> you the stranger? Or is the stranger the person you leave behind?

Sherm

P.S. Twenty-nine days to go.

PURELY VOLUNTARY

Bridge and Tab were standing outside Tab's apartment door, Tab feeling for her keys in her book bag, when the door was wrenched open from the inside. A hand seized Tab's wrist and another one grabbed Bridge's elbow. They were both dragged into the apartment.

"Celeste!" Tab shrieked. "What the—"

But Celeste just continued to drag them into the living room, where she pulled them both down onto the couch. The coffee table was piled with her school stuff: index cards, textbooks, spiral notebooks, and the laptop. Also a box of graham crackers.

"Celeste!" Tab shouted. "My shoes!" Because at Tab's everyone was supposed to take their shoes off by the front door.

Celeste grabbed the laptop and shoved it at them. "Look."

On the screen was a picture of Patrick, in his underwear. It was the same picture Em had shown Bridge back in November.

Bridge stared. "Why would he put that up there?"

"Duh," Celeste said. "He wouldn't."

"But—this is his page."

Celeste rolled her eyes. "Anyone with his phone could

have done it. Open the app, attach the picture, hit send, done. What I don't get is why he doesn't take it down."

Bridge glanced at the time in the corner of the screen. "He doesn't know. He's still at practice, probably."

"Look at how many people are commenting! He has fifty-seven likes!"

"I'd like to know why this is such a big deal," Tab said. "Look at what happened to Emily!"

"Trust me, it's a big deal." Celeste patted her sister on the head condescendingly. "If this is happening in middle school, I shudder to think what you guys are going to get up to in high school."

"*Us* guys?" Bridge said. "We didn't do this."

Tab said, "If it was posted from his phone, no one will ever know who did it, right?"

"They'll try, though," Celeste said. "They'll try to find out who did it."

"Well, now he knows what it feels like," Tab said.

"He doesn't know yet," Bridge said. "But he will soon."

Bridge's cell phone rang. "Em," she said, picking up. "I'm at Tab's. Yeah, we just saw it." There was a pause. "I know," Bridge said. "I know. But don't worry."

"What's she saying?" Tab hissed.

Bridge tilted the phone away from her mouth and said, "Em's worried it'll look like she did it. You know, to get him back."

"What?" Tab said. "That's stupid."

"It's not *that* stupid," Celeste said quietly. "The thought did cross my mind."

· · ·

An hour later, Bridge was almost home when she saw Alex crossing the street ahead of her.

"Hey!" she shouted. "Alex! Wait up."

Alex smiled when she caught up to him. "Hey, Bridge. Still with the ears, huh?"

She touched them reflexively. "Yeah, still with the ears."

"I guess you gotta be you."

They started walking toward home. "Listen," Bridge said. "What did Jamie bet you? He won't tell me."

His smile changed, widened. "I'm not surprised."

"Come on."

"Well," Alex drawled, "I probably don't have to tell you that your brother owns very little of value."

"That's my point," Bridge said. "Our parents won't let you take the laptop, you know."

Alex shook his head. "I don't want his laptop. What I ask is more of an—*entertainment.*"

"Spit it out," Bridge said. "What is it?"

"Fine. If he loses, he has to sing a song."

"That's it?"

"To Adrienne."

"Adrienne?"

"*Adrienne,*" he repeated, doing that obnoxious thing with his hands that meant a girl had a good body. "He has to sing to her. A whole song. In the middle of the Bean Bar. In his underwear."

"No way."

"Way." He leveled a look at her. "I put up a very valuable vintage T-shirt. He had to put something real on the line."

"Why are you trying to destroy Jamie? I thought you were his friend. Kind of." They walked into the building and crossed the lobby to wait for the elevator.

"I *am* his friend! We're having fun."

"Yeah, you're having fun crushing his soul."

The elevator door opened, and they got in.

"This is all purely voluntary, you know, Bridge. It's not my fault your brother loses every— Hey!"

Holding the elevator door open with one foot, Bridge had pushed the buttons for every floor in the building, except for sixteen, where Alex lived.

She pointed at the unlit button. "You can get that last one," she told him. Then she stepped back into the lobby and waved as the door closed between them. "Have fun!"

VALENTINE'S DAY

Maybe the human brain is slow to accept what it knows. Because you found yourself missing Vinny. You were in the habit of reaching for her—for her sharp edges, for her approval—the way you've been reaching for your phantom phone all day. Yes, she tried to humiliate Gina more than once. Yes, she tagged that mostly-naked selfie of Patrick McCormack so that every kid at the high school was sure to see it, even though it was pretty obvious he hadn't posted it on purpose. And Vinny and Patrick were actually friends last year in middle school. His whole account disappeared the next day. Poof.

In movies it always looks easy to turn away from the mean girl. That's what the audience wants you to do. But you couldn't stop thinking about everything you knew about Vinny, everything she knew about you. It hurt when she walked right past you every day, like a real, physical hurt. It felt like you were being erased. And time didn't make it any better.

For a solid month before Valentine's Day, everyone was all worked up about the carnations—a dollar a flower, to benefit the school library. The order forms were spilled all over a table just inside the school doors, index cards in three colors, white, pink, and red—along with paper clips to attach the dollar bills and a locked metal box with a slot in the top to drop them in.

White carnations for friendship. Pink for like. Red for love.

"Friendship, likeship, loveship!" Gina had joked.

Yesterday. Yesterday you walked into school and there Vinny was, bent over the table, filling out a card with her hair falling all over the table. Vinny, concentrating. Writing on a white card. For Zoe the Loyal?

At that moment you remembered Vinny's old wallpaper, the one she used to have when she was little, with carousels and clowns. You remembered the time you slept over and Vinny wanted to stay up "all night" even though you were only nine. You remembered how she dropped a glass on the kitchen floor at one a.m., how her dad came out and yelled, how her face went dead until it was over, how she walked straight back to her bed, turned to the wall, and pretended to be asleep. How was it possible that the two of you hadn't spoken in months?

"Hey," you said, taking a chance.

She turned. "Hey, you." She smiled and stood up, still holding her white card.

Relief flooded you like pure oxygen, and you inhaled it gratefully. You forgot about Vinny's smiles, how meaningless they are. The bell rang. You were already late for English.

"I miss you," Vinny said.

• • •

You cut first period together, just talking in the stairwell. You didn't talk about Gina or Zoe or anyone but the two of you. You talked about your third-grade teacher, and sleepovers at your house, and the time she cut your hair when you were eleven and it actually looked kind of amazing. Your mom told her she had a gift. When the five-minute bell rang, Vinny grabbed one of your hands, squeezed it, and said, "You know what? I think you're the only person in the world who really knows me." And it was as if a curtain went up and she was standing there—the old Vinny. Your Vinny. It felt like magic, like someone back from the dead.

That was when you told her Gina's secret. Vinny didn't even ask—you'd *wanted* to do it. That secret had been something that part of you had been waiting to give Vinny from the moment you heard it in Gina's bedroom. From the moment she whispered it into her own hands.

I can trust you, right?

The truthful answer would have been: not all of me.

When the words were coming out of your mouth—not just Marco's name, but the whole story—you felt like you were two different people. One of you was electrified by the power you wielded for the ninety seconds it took to say the words, the power to make Vinny truly happy. The other you watched, horrified, knowing that you'd just crossed a line that could never be uncrossed.

We're the kind who would never hurt each other.

You weren't that kind of friend anymore.

Of course, you had no idea about Vinny's plan. As you crossed the lobby together on the way to world history, Vinny stopped at the carnation table, picked up one of the blank cards—a red one—and began writing.

"To Marco," she said aloud as she wrote. "I couldn't think of another way to tell you how I really feel. I'm in love with you. Love, Gina." She had the dollar ready in her hand.

You tell yourself that if you had known what Vinny was planning, you would never have told her Gina's secret. Not in a million years.

But a million years is a long time.

GRAVITY

"Patrick's mom made him erase his account, and then she made him watch a documentary with her about cyberbullying," Em said, her breath billowing white in the cold air and then disappearing. "But she didn't take his phone. We still talk almost every night."

"So he knows you didn't do it, right?" Tab asked.

"He says he believes me. And I do have a pretty good alibi."

"You have witnesses!" Bridge said. Emily had been in the gym with the girls' JV soccer team when Patrick's photo was posted at 3:27 p.m.

"Yeah, twenty-five witnesses." Em smiled. "Including Patrick." The boys' team had been practicing too. "But you know, theoretically? I could have gone to the bathroom or something. That's probably what Mr. Ramos is thinking. Our backpacks were all piled up in the hall. Patrick's phone was right there."

Emily had a four o'clock meeting with Mr. Ramos. Her parents had been asked to attend. Even though it was freezing, Tab had talked them into going to the playground after school until Em had to leave. "Swings!" Tab had said. "Swings are the answer!"

Bridge didn't like swings. Everyone said swinging felt like flying, but Bridge felt the opposite. She would dutifully pump her legs, leaning forward and back, but mostly what she felt was the Earth's pull on her body. As if something were trying to drag her down.

"I'm surprised it took Mr. Ramos this long," Em said. "*Obviously* they think it's me. If I didn't know it wasn't me, I'd think it was me!"

"Em, anyone could have gone into his bag," Tab said. "Everyone knows what days you guys practice in the gym. Everyone knows where the bags will be."

"Good point," Em said. "Hey, if there's a trial, maybe you can be my lawyer, Tab. Right before they burn me at the stake or whatever."

"That's witches," Tab said.

"Close enough," Em said. "The boys on soccer are all giving me these poison looks, like they *know* I did it and think it's just the worst thing ever."

"It's exactly what happened to you!" Tab said, pumping her swing. "Now they know how it feels."

"Well, *they* don't know how it feels," Bridge said. "But Patrick does."

Em dragged her feet and stopped her swing. "And I actually feel even worse now than I did before. Which I didn't think was possible."

Still swinging, Tab looked at Em. "Well, if I were you, I'd feel great."

"Tab, Patrick is my actual friend now. Remember?"

"Just friends?" Bridge said.

"Yeah," Em said. "Friends." Then her phone rang, and she grinned. "Speak of the devil!"

She hopped off her swing and walked a few steps away. "Patrick?"

Tab shook her head. "Devil is right. Am I crazy, or is she completely deluded?"

"Remember when I got hit by the car?" Bridge said.

Tab's face changed. "Of course I remember." She slowed her swing.

"I don't," Bridge said. "Not really."

Tab started winding up her swing the way they did when they were little, turning herself with her feet so that the chain sides twisted together above her head, pulling her up inch by inch.

"I looked back to talk to you," Bridge said. "You were behind me."

"I know," Tab said, still turning. "I was there."

"I was going to yell 'Bug-buggy, zoo-buggy.'"

"You did yell it."

"I did?"

"Yes, right before you—went into the street."

"That's where I go blank."

"You're lucky," Tab said. After a few seconds she added, "Lucky in a way, I mean." She had wound her swing so high that her toes barely touched the ground.

Bridge looked at Tab. "What did it—look like?"

Tab closed her eyes. "Horrible. It looked horrible."

"Okay, but like—how, exactly?"

"The car hit you. You went up. You came down."

"Up? Like up in the air?"

Tab stared at Bridge. "You truly don't know this?"

Bridge shook her head.

"You flew. Up, up, up. And then you started coming down. But I didn't see—after that. I closed my eyes."

"You didn't see me land, you mean."

Tab shook her head.

"I wish I could have seen it," Bridge said.

"Bridge, it's not funny. It was really awful. It was the scariest day of my life."

Em came back. "I have to go. My parents are almost at school."

"Want us to walk you?" Tab asked.

"Nah, I'm good." Emily grabbed her bag from the sand at their feet. "Don't have fun without me." She walked toward the gate.

"Text us right after!" Bridge yelled.

When Em had gone, Tab said, "They talk every night?"

"Apparently," Bridge said.

Tab shook her head.

"Do you remember what color the car was?" Bridge asked. "That day?"

"The one that hit you?"

"No, the other one. The Bug."

"Yeah. It was yellow." Tab picked her feet up, and her swing unwound itself, spinning her hard. Bridge tried to watch but had to look away.

"Wait a minute," Bridge said. "So I definitely said 'Bug-buggy, zoo-buggy,' right? You heard me?"

Tab stopped spinning and planted her feet. "Yeah. Why?"

Bridge stood up. "That means . . ."

"What?"

"That means . . ."

Tab stared at her.

"That means I still owe you two punches!"

Tab leapt off her swing, laughing. "No! Get away!" She started running for the jungle gym, but she was dizzy, and Bridge got her before she reached it.

THE TRUTH ABOUT MOONLIGHT

Bridge's mom had always been there when she emerged from the mummy dream, throwing off her covers. Her mom had always been next to her while Bridge pictured the open sky and persuaded herself that she could move her arms and legs whenever she wanted to. She had always stayed close until Bridge was asleep again.

Not this time. This time, her mom was away, playing her cello at another wedding. This time, when Bridge had kicked her sheet and covers to the floor and taken her third deep breath, it was Jamie in the room with her, standing uncertainly near the door.

"You okay?" he asked.

"Yeah."

"You had the dream?"

"How did you know?" And for the first time Bridge wondered how her mother was able to always be there as she woke. She had never questioned it—her mother was her mother.

"There's a noise you make."

"Ew. A noise? Did it wake you up?"

"I was reading." Jamie rolled her desk chair toward the bed, but not too close, giving her lots of space. He sat. They could hear voices through the window, coming from the sidewalk below—talking, and a high peal of laughter.

"What time is it?" Bridge asked. The mummy dream usually came very late, when the whole world felt dead. She looked at the glowing numbers on her clock: it was only 11:48.

Bridge sat up. "Jamie! It isn't midnight yet. What about the bet?"

"Whatever. I'm so sick of that bet. You just gave me an excuse to be done with it."

"But—you mean that's it? Really? You lost? Because of me?"

"Yeah, I lost. Not because of you. Because of me."

"But now you—" She had been about to say "Now you have to sing to Adrienne in your underwear!" Instead, she said, "Now you'll never get your T-shirt back."

"Yeah. I should probably just buy the one on eBay. I'll save up."

"But you said only losers buy cool stuff on eBay."

He smiled. "So I'm a loser. Who cares?"

"I feel so bad. You could have stayed in bed—I would have been okay. I *am* okay."

"What does Mom do, when she comes in after the nightmare?"

"Just stays. But you don't have to. I'm fine."

"I can stay," Jamie said.

Bridge was quiet. She looked out the window, where a bright half-moon hovered above the buildings across the street. It was like a frosted cake, cut exactly down the middle.

Sherm said that there was no such thing as moonlight, that what she saw was just reflected light from the sun. But that seemed impossible.

"Jamie." Bridge could just make out his profile.

"Yeah?"

"After the accident. Do you think I lived for a reason?"

"Like one particular reason?"

"The nurse said that I must have lived for a reason."

He was quiet for a few seconds. "I think you're here for a lot of reasons, Bridge. But not that kind of reason."

"Oh."

"You know what Mom says: we're all just here to make music."

Bridge snorted. "Mom says everything is about music."

"But it's not actual music. She means like—we're here to be here. To live. That's why you lived, Bridge. You lived to live. Just like everyone else."

Just like everyone else. "You don't think I'm . . . different?"

Jamie laughed quietly. "You're definitely different."

"I *feel* different." Bridge had never put it into words before, but she wanted to, and the dark helped. "I feel like—like there's this part of me that nobody knows. And I don't know how it got there."

"Yeah," Jamie said. "We all have that."

Bridge was quiet. Everyone had that? "No, this came from the accident."

"What do you mean, it came from the accident?"

"I mean it showed up after that."

"Bridge, that was a long year. You spent a lot of time in

bed. Maybe it was the first time you stopped moving long enough to notice, but that voice in your head is called an inner life, and everybody has one. Except maybe Alex."

Bridge looked at the moon, and it seemed to look right back. "You think that's it?"

"Yeah. Everyone feels different on the inside. It doesn't mean you have a secret mission."

That made Bridge laugh.

"You really want to know why you lived?" Jamie said. "You lived because the doctors restarted your heart three times."

"Three times?"

"Yeah."

"No one ever told me that."

"Well, Mom and Dad probably didn't want to freak you out. Want me to open the window? The heat is really cranking."

"Okay," Bridge said, closing her eyes. "That'd be great." And a few moments later there was a wonderful rush of cold air, a smooth ribbon running along her cheek.

Jamie turned on her desk lamp and settled back into the chair with his book. "I'll read in here for a while. Okay, Rudolph? We'll be independent together."

She felt sleep tug at her. "You wouldn't mind my red nose?"

"Not if you don't mind me being a dentist."

Sleepily, she smiled. "It's a deal."

VALENTINE'S DAY

You're sitting by the window watching a guy with a bucket of roses set up shop near the subway station. Each flower is individually wrapped in cellophane and tied with a red ribbon, and he's got a sign that says $3 that he props up against the bucket.

By now, everyone at school has clocked everyone else's carnations—how many, which colors, et cetera. Vinny probably has at least six. Zoe the Loyal has at least one white one, from Vinny. Gina has the three white flowers you sent her and wonders where you were at lunch and doesn't yet know that Marco will avoid her after school, or why.

If your mom were here, she would tell you that none of this is so terrible. She'd say that she remembers being young. That high school is complicated. That friends are complicated. That none of it is as important as it feels. That's why you aren't calling her. Because if she truly remembered, she'd know that everything is exactly as terrible as it feels. She'd sit down right next to you and say, "It's bad."

She'd probably also say that mental-health days require a parent signature. She'd say you put her and your father through a hell full of worry. You did. You are.

You turn around and call to Adrienne, who's practicing her footwork while she refills the milk canisters next to the coffee lids. Somehow she doesn't spill a drop. "Hey," you say. "Where is Mr. Barsamian, anyway?"

"He had to go—family emergency, he said."

"Family emergency?" You stand up. "What happened?"

"Oh, not his family," Adrienne says. "But someone's kid is missing, a friend of the family." She glances up, sees your face. "No," she says. "No way."

Ten minutes later, you've talked Adrienne down. Her original plan was to turn you in immediately, but you've promised to go straight home. Your last lie, you tell yourself.

You pull your hoodie on. "I hate to ask this," you tell Adrienne. "But can I borrow three dollars?"

BLACK LINES

Backstage, playing spit, Bridge looked at Sherm and thought about his bread smell and how it was a little bit sweet. Lately it reminded Bridge of the cold, frothy antibiotics she took as a little kid. She'd had so many throat infections that the smell of it—"pink drink," her father called it—became part of her childhood, like music she barely noticed during a scene in a movie. Sherm's bread smell was the same, except that it was always at the front of her brain, something she urgently did and did not want to talk about. None of it exactly made sense.

Tab's head appeared through the opening in the curtain. "Em's officially off the hook. Mr. Ramos says she didn't do it."

"Woot!" Bridge high-fived Tab, then Sherm.

"I'm skipping Hindi Club to celebrate," Tab said, sinking to the floor next to Bridge. "Can I hide out here with you guys?"

"Sure." Sherm stuffed his sandwich wrapper into his bag. "You can keep Bridge company until the bell rings."

"You're leaving?" Bridge said.

He nodded. "I got a note. I have to talk to Mr. Ramos in five minutes."

"Now *you're* a suspect?" Tab said.

He shrugged. "Or maybe they think I'm the official school narc."

"You're not a narc," Tab said seriously. "You're just a dork. The good kind."

"Yeah." He smiled. "I know."

Watching him disappear into the red curtain, Bridge was struck by the knowledge that Sherm was the main thing she looked forward to every day. How had that happened?

Bridge had once believed that state borders were something you could see, actual black lines that you could walk along if you wanted to, one foot in front of the other. Then, when she was seven, she'd demanded the window seat on a plane trip to see her grandparents in California, telling Jamie that she wanted to see *exactly when* they crossed from one state to the next.

"But how will you know?" Jamie had asked, looking actually interested.

"The black lines!" she told him.

And he had laughed, of course.

There was no black line separating Colorado from Utah. There was no black line between friendship and whatever might come next. And Bridge didn't know whether she would want to step over that line, if there were one.

Tab had opened a bag of chips and was eating them one at a time, looking weirdly solemn, as if she felt sorry for them.

"How are you supposed to know what you want?" Bridge asked her.

"About Sherm, you mean?"

"Yeah." Bridge felt herself flush. Tab always picked up on more than she let on. "What do you think the Berperson would say?"

"Well," Tab said, perking up, "the Berperson says the most important thing is to be true to yourself."

"But what's 'yourself'? That's the problem. What if I don't know?"

Tab shrugged. "Then I guess you should just . . . be true." She wiped potato-chip salt on her jeans.

"Gee, thanks," Bridge said. "Super-helpful."

The bell rang. Tab stood up and put both hands out to pull Bridge to her feet. "You want to know what I think?"

"Yeah. But please don't tell me to put a pin in it."

"I think that when you don't know, you should just wait until you do."

Bridge smiled. "That actually makes sense."

"Yeah," Tab said, feeling for the opening in the curtain. "In other words, put a pin in it."

SHERM

January 27

Dear Nonno Gio,

No one gets picked up after school in seventh grade. It was pretty easy to spot you out there, scanning the steps with one hand over your eyes like a salute.

I just turned around and went out through the yard gate instead. I guess you thought maybe I'd run right up to you and we'd go get a slice like we used to.

I know it's only been five months, but you look smaller. I'm not just saying that to be mean. Otherwise you seem the same. It was good to see you, but it also felt good to walk away. Now you know how it feels.

Sherm

P.S. Eighteen days.

THE PITFALLS OF BEING
WONDER WOMAN

The next morning, Sherm was on the corner in his down vest and navy-blue thermal shirt, which was Bridge's favorite. He gave her a funny smile as she walked toward him.

"What?"

He pointed. "Stove Top stuffing? Is that breakfast?"

"Oh." She realized she was cradling the cardboard canister as if it were a baby. "No, this is for Tab. She has to get some teeth pulled today. She's leaving at lunchtime."

"Bleh."

"Yeah," Bridge said. "My mom gave me this to give to her—she says it's the best thing to eat after you've had a tooth pulled."

"They should put that on their ads." Sherm made his voice low, like a television announcer's: "Stove Top. Really great for after the dentist!"

They laughed. Then Bridge replayed it in her head and laughed harder. Then she couldn't stop laughing.

"Are you one of those people who laughs really hard at bad jokes?" Sherm asked. "How did I not know that?"

When Bridge powered up her phone after school, it began to ding with voice-mail messages. When it stopped, she had six of them, all from Tab. She didn't bother listening to them, but texted Tab instead:

Bridge: U OK?

Tab: There U R! Come see me??

Bridge: At home?

Tab: No! Still at bad dentist. ☹☹☹

Bridge and Tab both went to Dr. Miller, and they'd called him "bad dentist" since they were little kids. He was only eight blocks from school.

Tab: U coming?

Tab: Come now?

Bridge was supposed to be at a Tech Crew meeting in ten minutes. The Talentine show was Friday, and Mr. Partridge had been telling them for days that it was crunch time.

Tab: U there? U coming?

Bridge: Yes! Coming!

Tab: K. Love U. ☺☺☺

Bridge: Love U too.

Tab: ☺☺☺☺☺☺☺☺

Ten minutes later, Tab was resting on Bridge's shoulder in the waiting room, talking and crying through a mouth full of cotton while the receptionist pretended not to look at them.

"And then, thith morning I told her what I did, and she thaid . . . she thaid I have to *tell*. That'th part of it, she thaid!"

"Part of what?" Bridge said. "Tab, I don't know what you're talking about. You started in the middle."

"Didn't you get my voith mailth?"

"I didn't have time to listen to any of them! I just ran over here."

"Bridth?"

"What?"

"I like your earth."

"My earth? Tab, you're not making sense."

Her head still resting on Bridge's shoulder, Tab reached up and felt for Bridge's cat ears. She patted them awkwardly. "Your eeerth!" she said.

"Oh, my *ears*." Bridge removed Tab's hand from her head. "That's nice. But I still have no idea what you're talking about. Who do you have to tell what? And why?"

"I'm talking about thivil dithobedienth! She thaid I have to 'take rethponthibility'!" Tab sat up and looked urgently at Bridge.

Bridge stared at her. "Who said?"

"The Berperthon! Bridth, I pothted the naked picthur of Patrick." She pounded her chest with an open hand. "From hith phone, during thoccer practith." She mimed texting with her thumbs.

"Wait," Bridge said. "You're saying—it was you?"

Tab nodded miserably. "I'm going to get thuthpended!" she wailed.

"No, you're not."

"Yeth, I am! And I have to tell Em," Tab said, waving the spitty paper towel she had balled up in one hand.

"Wow. She's gonna flip."

Tab nodded and then closed her eyes.

Bridge patted Tab's face carefully. "It's going to be okay."

Tab nodded and said, "You're the betht."

"Tab? Where's your mom?"

"Getting the car. Come over?"

"Your mom won't mind?"

Tab shook her head. "I need you, Bridth."

An hour later, Bridge and Tab stood in Tab's small kitchen, eating mini-marshmallows and waiting for the Stove Top to cook.

"Text Emily again." Tab's face was smaller without the cotton in her mouth. "Where *is* she?"

"I texted her four times," Bridge said.

"Then check your phone."

"I've *been* checking it, Tab. If I get a text, we'll hear it."

Tab stirred her Stove Top slowly. "She's going to hate me."

"She's not going to hate you."

"How do you know?"

"We have a rule, remember? No fights."

"That's true." Tab looked a little bit hopeful.

"So when's your mom getting here with your antibiotics?" Bridge glanced at the bag of marshmallows.

"With the hot chocolate, you mean?"

"Yeah. The way you're plowing through those, there won't be any left."

Tab stuffed two more into her mouth and said, "Tough."

Then Bridge's phone dinged, and Tab dove for it.

"Too late!" Bridge snatched it. "Ha. Those dentist drugs are slowing you down."

Em: **No WAY I'm coming over—I officially hate Tab.**

Bridge: What? Why?????

Em: Guess what? TAB posted that picture of P. Total triator.

Em: *Traitor!

Bridge: Who told you? Please come!

Em: She told me! She was LAUGHING. No way.

"What's she saying?" Tab said. "Is she coming?"

"Tab. I think you may have called Emily from the dentist's office."

"What? No, I didn't."

"Are you sure?"

Tab spent the next ten minutes crying on the kitchen floor while the Stove Top burned. Bridge hadn't seen Tab cry this much in her whole life. It was awful. Then the doorbell rang.

"It's freezing out," Em said, marching past Bridge. "Where is she?"

"You came," Tab said. She'd managed to get up from the floor and was standing next to the couch, holding the bag of marshmallows.

Em hesitated. "You look terrible," she said. "Are you okay? Never mind. Sit down. I have a present for you."

"A present?" Tab looked confused. She sat down on the couch.

"A whole *bunch* of presents," Em said. She sat on the coffee table in her coat, pulled her backpack onto her lap, unzipped the smallest front pocket, and pulled out a handful of torn paper. "Hold out your hand."

They were notes. Em put them into Tab's hand, one at a time.

Slut.

Rat.

You suck.

"Oh, and here's my favorite," Em said. "'Skank.' That kind of says it all, I think. Don't you agree?"

Tab looked stunned. "Where did these come from?"

"My locker. I actually prefer this to being hissed at in the hall, if you want to know the truth."

"But—when did it start?" Tab asked.

"Why? Do you actually care about someone other than the Berperson and her special rules of life?"

Tab looked like she was about to cry again. Bridge couldn't stand it. "Come on, Em," she said.

Em sighed and, still wearing her coat, lay back on the coffee table. "I got a couple of them after Sherm got all the boys in trouble—I figure that was David Marcel, mad about getting suspended. But they really started coming after *someone* posted Patrick's selfie."

"Idiots." Bridge scooped the notes out of Tab's hand, crunched them up, and dumped them on the table.

Tab sank back into the couch. "I feel—so, *so* terrible, Em. It was supposed to be civil disobedience. Like we talked about in Human Rights Club."

Emily laughed. "I think you should reread that chapter or something."

They heard the key in the door, and Tab's face changed. "My parents don't know yet," she whispered. "Don't say anything."

But it was only Celeste. She came into the living room, blinking snow off her eyelashes.

"No way, it's snowing?" Emily said, without getting up. "Finally! A decent development in this sucky day."

Celeste looked at Tab's face, then stared at Em, who was still lying across the coffee table like a sacrifice. She stepped a little closer and squinted at the pile of notes lying next to her. Bridge hadn't managed to crunch them very well, and they were mostly legible. "What's going on?" Celeste said. "And what's that *smell?*"

"I lost one of my two best friends," Tab said flatly. "And I'm going to get suspended. Burnt stuffing."

"No, you didn't," Em said. "And you're not going to get suspended."

"Tab, what are you talking about?" Celeste said.

Tab stamped her foot on the rug. "Boys are evil."

"What do you mean, *suspended?*" Celeste said.

So Tab confessed, for the fourth time that day.

"Okay, you guys, back up," Celeste said. "Back up all the way to the beginning."

They started with Patrick's first text to Emily, and they told Celeste everything. Tab finished by describing her meeting with the Berperson that morning, how the Berperson was "so weirdly upset" and said Tab had "exactly twenty-four hours" to tell Mr. Ramos that she was the person who'd posted the picture of Patrick.

Tab wiped her nose with a wad of paper towel she found in her pocket. "You hate me now, right, Em? We can't be friends anymore."

Em looked at Tab. "What's wrong with you? Of course we're still going to be friends."

243

"You said you *hate* me."

"I was mad. It's called a *fight*. Jeez."

"But we don't have fights," Tab said. "Ever."

"Well, maybe we should learn."

Tab's eyes got big. "Learn to *fight*? What about our rule? What about the Twinkie?"

Em carefully tore a marshmallow into two pieces and handed one to Tab. "With this marshmallow, I hereby release you from the Twinkie promise."

Behind Em, Bridge was mouthing two words to Tab.

Tab sat forward and tilted her head, trying to read her lips. "What? Say what?"

"Say you're *sorry*!" Bridge said.

"Oh! Didn't I say that? Em, I'm sorry! I'm so, so sorry." She popped the half marshmallow into her mouth.

Em laughed. "You guys are a good team."

"It still isn't fair," Tab said. "I just wanted Patrick to know how it felt! How it felt for *you*, when he sent your picture to everyone."

"*How* many times do I have to tell you?" Em said. "Patrick didn't send my picture to anyone!"

Tab rolled her eyes. "Em, please don't tell me again about how someone grabbed his phone."

"Someone did grab his phone!" Em said.

"Really? Who?"

"I told you, I don't know! But I believe him, Tab. Listen, I didn't know him before. You guys were right about that, okay? But I know him now. Can't you take my word for it?"

Tab shook her head. "I can't take your word for it if you're taking his word for it."

Celeste had been unusually quiet through the whole story. Even when she heard about the knee-length shorts, her expression didn't change. Now she said, "Emily, I think I know who grabbed Patrick's phone and sent your picture to David Marcel."

"You do?" All three of them looked at Celeste.

"How well do you guys know Julie Hopper?"

Tab exploded. "Julie Hopper! She's a—girl! Why would she send Em's picture to a boy? To *David Marcel?*"

Celeste laughed. "What? You don't think girls hurt girls? Tab, you live in a dreamworld."

"I do not!" Tab looked at Emily and Bridge. "Right, you guys?"

And then Celeste started crying.

The girls pushed close to her, patting Celeste's snow-damp hair and not asking questions. After a minute, Celeste took the paper towel Tab held out and blotted her face with it. "Sorry," she said. "It's been a crap week."

"Oh my God, you guys," Em said. "Oh my God. Celeste is right." She held out her phone. She'd been texting with one hand while patting Celeste's shoulder with the other.

Emily: **Hey**

Patrick: **Hey U**

Emily: **Question for U**

Patrick: **?**

Emily: **Did JH send the picture to DM?**

Patrick: **...**

Emily: **Is that a yes?**

Patrick: **...**

Emily: **?**

Patrick: yeah

Emily: SERIOUSLY?

Patrick: ☹

Emily: ??? WHAT IS WRONG WITH HER?

Patrick: Issues.

Patrick: ☹

Tab clutched the phone, frantically rereading. "Wait. Patrick *didn't* send your picture to anyone?" She looked from Em's face to Bridge's. "I actually *deserve* to get suspended."

"I didn't believe him either," Bridge said.

"And for the last time," Em said, "you are *not* going to get suspended!"

Celeste pushed her hand into the bag of marshmallows. "Oh yes, she is. She's totally going to get suspended."

OUTLAWS

Celeste was right again. When Tab explained everything to Mr. Ramos the next morning, he suspended her for three days.

"Starting Monday," Tab told Em and Bridge at lunch. "And get this: I'm kicked out of the Talentine show."

"What?" Bridge said. For some reason she felt tears threatening.

"Yeah, I can't be in it. I'm still allowed to go, though, because it's on Friday and I'm not suspended until next week—so, Em, will you be my date?"

"Of course I'll be your date," Em said. "We'll sit front row center."

"Or maybe *back* row center," Tab said. "The two of us should probably lie low for the rest of the year."

"Lie low?" Em made her hands into guns. "Who are we, Bonnie and Clyde?"

Tab made a face. "According to my parents? Yes. We might as well have robbed a bank."

"Okay," Em said. "We'll sit in the back."

"Did I tell you guys about this flower-delivery thing they do at Celeste's high school on Valentine's Day?" Tab shook her head. "It's sadistic. All the popular people walk around with a million flowers and everyone else feels like crap."

"Jamie's school does that too," Bridge said. "Isn't it a fundraiser for the library or something? Maybe it's not so bad."

"It's terrible!" Tab said. "When I get to high school? I'm gonna start a petition against it. Freshman year."

Em and Bridge looked at each other. "What happened to lying low?" Em said.

"I am lying low!" Tab said. "But that's just for now."

When Bridge got home after Tech Crew, there was a flyer taped above the elevator button in the lobby.

SPECIAL DEBUT TONIGHT!
Our own Jamie Barsamian
aka "J-Bar"
performing
@ the Bean Bar
6:30 p.m.
NOT TO BE MISSED

She read it four times before the meaning sank in. Then she turned and ran.

HAPPY BIRTHDAY

When Bridge shoved open the door of the Bean Bar, Alex and Jamie were already there—Alex smiling, Jamie, in jeans and a black long-sleeved shirt, looking at his feet. Alex was wearing Jamie's Rolling Stones T-shirt.

Bridge felt a surge of frustration. She needed a plan. And maybe a cookie.

Adrienne was behind the cash register. "Hey there, Finnegan."

"My dad's not here, is he?" Bridge asked.

Adrienne shook her head. "I think he's getting your mom at the airport. Hey, who's that kid with your brother?"

"That's Alex."

"Is he your brother's friend? Because he's always coming in here and asking me out. He's what, fifteen? It's creepy."

Bridge smiled. "I'll tell him you said that." She wondered if she should warn Adrienne that Jamie was possibly about to take off his clothes and sing her a song. Then she noticed Jamie, sitting on a chair and calmly taking off one of his sneakers. The other one was already on the floor.

She ran up to him. "Are you sure you have to do this?"

Jamie smiled. "A bet's a bet. Are you sure you want to be here?" He stood up and undid the button of his jeans.

"Wait—I want to help. Maybe I have something Alex would take instead. I have that weird purple crystal Mom brought me from New Mexico. Maybe we could tell him it has, like, powers or something."

"Hey!" Jamie called over to Alex, who was standing near a couple of kids he'd obviously talked into coming. "Instead of me doing this, you want a weird purple crystal from New Mexico?"

"No thanks." Alex grinned like a drunk pirate. Bridge wanted to kick him.

"Didn't think so." Jamie started peeling off his jeans.

"Jamie!" Bridge yelled, which only attracted attention. Several people turned to look at him.

"Thanks for that," Jamie said. And in one motion, he brought his jeans to his ankles.

That was when Bridge finally shut up. Because underneath his jeans, Jamie was wearing his heavy-duty long underwear. The thick black ones he wore camping. They looked a lot like running pants.

"Hey!" Alex called. "We said 'underwear'!"

"Yeah." Jamie smiled. "But we didn't say what kind. Check your contract." He folded his jeans neatly, stacked them on his chair, and then, dressed head to toe in black, walked over to Adrienne.

She cocked her head and did an up-down gesture with one finger. "What's this?"

"I'm going to sing 'Happy Birthday' to you," Jamie said. "It's the shortest song I know. Please don't hit me or call the police." He went down on one knee.

Adrienne crossed her arms.

And then Jamie sang "Happy Birthday" to Adrienne. It took about ten seconds.

When he was done, a few people clapped. Jamie bowed once, walked back to his clothes, and started getting dressed.

Alex was trying to look smug, though Bridge was pretty sure he'd had something a lot more humiliating in mind. She couldn't wait to tell him that Adrienne thought he was creepy.

Bridge walked up to Adrienne, who was still standing there. "He lost a bet," Bridge explained.

"To the creep?"

Bridge nodded.

Adrienne looked over at Jamie and Alex. "It's not my birthday!" she called.

"It's not?" Alex said. "But I thought all angels were born on Valentine's Day!"

Idiot, Bridge thought. Adrienne wasn't the type to fall for a stupid line. And anyway, Valentine's Day wasn't until Friday.

Adrienne glared at Alex. Then she came out from behind the counter and walked right toward him with a furious look on her face, bouncing on her toes a little with each step. Bridge enjoyed the way all the confidence drained out of Alex's smile. He looked like he was fighting the urge to run. But at the last second, Adrienne turned to Jamie, took his face in her hands, and kissed him on both cheeks.

"Thanks for the song," she said. "I enjoyed it. Kind of."

Jamie smiled and said, "I also brought you this. It's a birthday present. Kind of." He held out a closed hand and dropped something into Adrienne's hand. It took Bridge a couple of seconds to realize what it was.

Adrienne smiled. "Who's this?"

"That's Hermey," Jamie said. "He's an elf who wants to be a dentist."

"Man," Alex said. "You are so *weird*."

Jamie turned to him. "You can't fire me," he said. "I quit."

THE SECOND DEFINITION
OF PERMISSION

Bridge and Jamie walked home together in a sharp wind that froze Bridge's nose. She cupped her hands over her face. "Why didn't you explain the whole thing to Adrienne ahead of time? I told you she boxes. She might have actually hit you!"

Jamie smiled at her. He seemed not to feel the cold. "It would have been a violation of the contract."

Bridge dropped her hands. "There's really a contract?"

"Yep." Jamie was walking quickly, and Bridge had to jog a little to keep up.

"You could have told her anyway. He wouldn't have found out."

"It was better this way. You know what someone said once? It's easier to ask for forgiveness than it is to get permission."

"Huh." Bridge wasn't sure she got it.

"Which reminds me." Jamie pointed with one thumb over his shoulder at his backpack. "I stole another rock for your fake moon."

Bridge and Sherm had been lugging rocks to school for two weeks, trying to make a moon floor for the Talentine show. Mr. Partridge had said it was okay to take rocks from the park as long as they returned them later.

When they got home, Jamie showed up in Bridge's room holding a large gray rock with jagged edges.

"Wow, nice one." Bridge added it to the pile next to her desk. "Thanks."

"Thanks for being there tonight," Jamie said. "I didn't think I wanted anyone to see me, but it was nice. Like I had someone on my team, you know?"

Bridge almost said, "Hey, what do you say we both be independent together, huh?" Instead, she grabbed her backpack from the floor, pulled out two soft black bundles, and tossed one to Jamie. "I got you something too."

He shook it out and held it up in front of him.

It wasn't the official Rolling Stones 1981 North American Tour shirt. It was just a black T-shirt with one word across the back: CREW.

Bridge held up her own shirt. "See? They match."

Jamie smiled. "Thanks, Bridge. I think it might be my new favorite T-shirt."

She grinned at him. "It was the least I could do. You paid for them."

He threw his T-shirt at her. "Hey," she said, removing it from her head. "You gave Hermey away."

"Yeah," Jamie said. "It was time."

Bridge made her face serious, put her hand over her heart, and recited her number-one favorite Rudolph line: "'Goodbye, Hermey. Whatever a dentist is, I hope, someday, you'll be the greatest.'"

She was almost asleep that night when she heard her mom's cello, low and beautiful. Then the music stopped, and she heard her parents' murmuring voices, and Jamie's. After a minute, Jamie laughed loudly. She hadn't heard him really laugh in a long time. She rolled over and stared for a while into the box of rocks on the floor next to her bed. Then she reached for her phone and texted Emily: **Start practicing. You're singing on Friday.**

Em texted back right away: **???**

Bridge: **Trust me.**

Then she dialed Sherm. "You awake?"

"Yeah. Hi."

"Have you ever heard this thing about forgiveness and permission?"

"Mmm."

"Sherm?"

"Actually, I lied. I wasn't awake."

"Oh. Sorry. But listen."

SHERM

February 12

Dear Nonno Gio,
    Here are the answers to the texts you sent me this week:

1. Yes, I know there was a supermoon on Wednesday. It was too cloudy to see anything, so I doubt that you looked at it and thought about me.
2. I don't believe that your heart is in pieces. I think if your heart were in pieces, you would be dead. I can double-check with Dad if you want.
3. I know you miss me and you're sorry that everything is different. Me too.

                                     Sherm

P.S. Two days till the big day.

VALENTINE'S DAY

Who's the real you? The person who did something awful, or the one who's horrified by the awful thing you did? Is one part of you allowed to forgive the other?

Adrienne sends you home with three dollars and an extra-large hot chocolate. She doesn't hug you or even really say goodbye, but you can see her watching you, standing at the window with her arms crossed, until you walk away.

FIVE

THE OTHER DOOR

On Valentine's Day, Bridge met Sherm on their usual corner. Each of them carried a box of rocks.

"I was hoping you'd have a cart or something," Bridge said. "My fingers are getting numb." She tried to wiggle them without dropping the box and could barely feel anything. "Whose dumb idea was it to collect a mountain of rocks?"

Sherm smiled. They both knew it had been Bridge's idea. They started toward school.

"Hey, remember that riddle with the two brothers and the doors to heaven and hell?" Bridge said.

"Yeah."

"I asked my brother. He says the one question you have to ask is 'What door would your *brother* say is the door to heaven?'"

"But which brother do you ask?" Sherm leaned into Bridge a little bit as they walked. She glanced at his box and realized it held a lot more rocks than hers did. Maybe he didn't know he was leaning into her?

"It doesn't matter which one you ask. Either one will point you to the wrong door."

"Really?"

"Yeah, because the liar will lie about what his brother would say, which is the truth. And the truthful brother will tell you the truth about what the liar would say, which is a lie."

"So you get the wrong answer no matter what," Sherm said.

"Yeah," Bridge said happily. "Whichever door they tell you is the one to heaven, you just pick the other one."

"There's Patrick," Sherm said, just as Patrick saw them and waved.

"Let me get that," he said, scooping up Bridge's heavy box. Tab would have had a fit, but Bridge just shook out her sore arms and said thanks.

Patrick smiled at her. "Your ears are crooked."

"Oh!" Bridge felt for them and realized they were almost falling off.

Sherm smiled into his box of rocks. "I was going to tell you. But it looked kind of cute."

"Em's been practicing," Patrick said. "She's good."

"I know, right?" Bridge smiled at him. "So good."

Sherm looked at Patrick. "Let's drop the rocks off backstage. Mr. Partridge said we could use the side door." He turned to Bridge. "You coming?"

"There's Tab," Bridge said, pointing. "I'll go in with her."

He nodded. "See you at lunch?"

"Yeah."

The line of kids waiting outside the school doors was longer than usual, even though it was freezing. The teachers and staff always stayed late the night before Valentine's Day, decorating the school according to the secret Talentine theme. Bridge and Sherm and everyone on Tech Crew had stayed late too, helping with the decorations and finishing the set for the show. Before the night was over, Mr. Partridge had ordered at least six pizzas.

When Bridge and Tab crowded in together, the first things they saw were Sherm's banners, hanging over their heads:

REACH FOR THE STARS!

TAKE OFF AT THE TALENTINE SHOW! 5 P.M. TODAY!

And Bridge's favorite, hanging over the bake-sale table:

HOUSTON, WE HAVE CUPCAKES.

Tab clapped and jumped up and down. "Outer space! I knew you guys would pick a cool theme."

"It's not outer space," Bridge said. "It's supposed to be Apollo 11. The moon landing, remember? One giant step for humankind?"

"Look!" Tab pointed. "Pretty!"

There were silver stars hanging up and down the hallway behind the cafeteria, swaying just over their heads. When Bridge looked more closely, she saw that each star had a paper heart glued to its center, with writing on it.

Love is the most powerful emotion.

Love is the answer to the world's problems. It's about being vulnerable.

Love is when your heart wraps around something and won't let go.

They were all definitions of love.

"Yikes," Bridge said. "I didn't see these last night. I think this is that horrible homework assignment we did in the fall." She looked more closely. "They cut up our papers! Isn't that illegal or something?"

Tab clapped again. "Let's look for ours!"

"No," Bridge said. She happened to be within arm's length of her own definition—she could read it from where they stood:

Love is when you like someone so much that you can't just call it "like," so you have to call it "love."

Bridge shuddered. "At least they didn't put our names on them."

"I'm going to guess which one is yours," Tab said, running in the wrong direction.

"Ick," Bridge called after her. "Don't!"

Tab circled back to her. "Bridge, we'll send each other carnations on Valentine's Day, right? In high school? Like Celeste told us about?"

"What about your petition?"

"Yeah, I mean if I *don't* do the petition. I'm going to send you all three—white, pink, *and* red. Because you're my friend, and I like you, and I love you. Emily, too."

Bridge smiled. "I'm going to send you two of each."

SINGING HER SONG

The Talentine-show plan felt elaborate, but it wasn't. That was what Sherm kept saying. "Nothing will go wrong. Just remember to run for the lights."

Every time an act finished, two or three Tech Crew kids ran onstage, carrying microphones and music stands, dragging extension cords, folding chairs, amplifiers—racing to set up whatever the next performers needed and take away whatever they didn't. It sounded easy, but there were a hundred little things to remember—one eighth grader was short and needed her mike stand set up very low; the amplifiers had to face out, couldn't be too close to the speakers, and had different ways of plugging in; and half of the music stands broke into two parts if you tried to carry them with one hand. Bridge had already done that twice, in front of the whole audience.

They'd decided that Em would sing last. Bridge and Sherm made sure they weren't assigned to break down the last "official" act, which was a barbershop quartet of eighth graders.

All Em needed was a microphone, a stand, and a spotlight. Sherm would carry the microphone, spooling out the cord the way Mr. Partridge taught them, and Emily, pretending to be Bridge, would carry the mike stand. It was pretty dim onstage when the lights were off, and with Emily wearing Bridge's cat ears and Jamie's black CREW T-shirt as a disguise, not even the other Tech Crew kids would realize what was happening until it was too late.

Once the microphone was set up, Sherm would run off-stage, leaving Em to sing her song. Meanwhile, Bridge would get to the lights.

"This one," Sherm had told her the day before, flipping a switch back and forth. "Just a spotlight, set to hit center stage. That's where I'll leave her."

Backstage, when Bridge put her ears on Em's head, Em looked at her and said, "I don't know if I can do this." The barbershop quartet was working up to its big finish. Bridge had heard the acts all week at rehearsal and knew most of them by heart.

"You can do it," Bridge said automatically. She was watching Sherm drag a bundle of microphone cord toward the stage, measuring with his eyes how much they would need.

"No," Em said. "You don't understand. I actually have no idea what kind of sound is going to come out of my mouth. I'm scared."

Bridge glanced at Em's legs—she was wearing a black skirt and black tights. "Are your legs shaking?" she said.

"I'm falling apart," Em said. "That's what I'm trying to tell you!"

"You're not falling apart," Bridge said. "You're scared."

"Isn't that the same thing?"

"No."

Someone came up behind Em and knocked on the wall

tentatively. It was Patrick. Em turned and smiled. "Hey, you." She went over and pressed into him, exhaling into his shoulder. "Bridge says being scared and falling apart aren't the same thing, but I think she's full of it."

"She's not full of it," Patrick said. "And you're going to be great."

Em took two fingers and hooked one of his thumbs, squeezing. Bridge caught herself staring and looked over at Sherm. Then the quartet sang its last note, the audience started clapping, and the three tech kids assigned to break down the last act sprinted onstage in their black T-shirts like a SWAT team. Mr. Partridge had been timing their setups and breakdowns all week. He said anything over twenty-five seconds was "simply unprofessional."

"Now or never," Sherm said quietly.

Em stood straight, turned her back on Patrick, and adjusted the cat ears. "I know why you like these," she told Bridge. "They're nice."

Bridge said, "So just friends, huh? You and Patrick?"

Em smiled. "I didn't say just friends forever."

"Seriously," Sherm said. "Now or never."

Em let herself be hugged by Bridge, and then she followed Sherm onto the dim stage. Bridge listened to the audience get quiet, probably checking their programs, before she remembered that she was supposed to be sprinting toward the lights.

When Bridge got to the light board at the back of the auditorium, breathing hard, Mr. Partridge was standing in front of it, scowling at the cue sheet.

Bridge's heart felt like a fist with no air in it. Onstage, she could make out Sherm's bent form taping down the microphone cord, and she could see the flat of Em's face, tilted toward the people in the seats, who had begun to shift and talk in the dark.

"Not on the program," Mr. Partridge said, looking at Bridge.

"No," Bridge said. She saw Sherm scoot away, leaving Emily in front of the microphone, alone. The talking in the audience was getting louder.

Bridge reached out and flipped Sherm's switch. A circle of light broke over Emily, who winced and shaded her eyes with one hand. The audience got quiet again, and Bridge waited to be screamed at by Mr. Partridge.

"Sorry," she whispered.

But Mr. Partridge seemed to have forgotten all about her. He was looking at the stage. He narrowed his eyes at Em and flipped another switch. The cone of harsh light around her became gentler, warmer. Em dropped her hand. Her shoulders unhunched, and her face relaxed.

"See that?" Mr. Partridge said to Bridge. "That's us, up there with her. I hit a switch, and just like that, she knows she's not alone."

He turned and gave Bridge the tiniest smile before looking back to the stage. And she got this picture in her head, so clear it could have been a memory, of Mr. Partridge waiting patiently in line at Nussbaum's for the Banana Splits Book Club's black-and-white cookies. She had a feeling that black-and-white cookies were not in the school budget.

On the stage, Em pulled off Bridge's ears and bent down to lay them at her feet. Then she stood up straight and looked out. Bridge remembered what it had been like to stand where Emily was standing, facing the rows of seats. And for the first time she was scared for her.

She glanced at Mr. Partridge. "We're here," he said, and Bridge realized he was talking to Em. "It's okay. Sing to the people."

And, as if she could hear him, Emily opened her mouth and sang. She sang just as beautifully as she had at her audition, with that same twist of nakedness and power. But this time Em didn't sing to the wall. She sang to every person in the room.

It was another one of those moments: like sitting in the backseat of the car with Tab, smelling burnt marshmallows; like the first few notes of her mother's cello music in the morning; like sitting cross-legged on the floor backstage, splitting the deck to play another game of spit with Sherm.

Standing next to Mr. Partridge in the dark, she remembered the face of the nurse at the hospital, more clearly than she had in years: "You must have been put on this earth for a reason, little girl."

Bridge knew why she was here. It's why we're all here, she thought.

Call it Mr. Partridge with his black-and-white cookies. Call it Em standing on that stage with her knees shaking but her voice strong. Call it Jamie looking awkward in the doorway of her bedroom after she'd had the mummy nightmare. Call it love.

"Are all those pizzas we've been eating really in the budget?" she whispered to Mr. Partridge.

He looked down at her, surprised. "I'll tell you a secret," he said. "Pretty much nothing is in the budget."

And then the audience burst into applause.

I THINK I SEE YOU TOO

Em didn't win any prizes at the Talentine show.

"You should have!" Patrick said, after. "You were top three, for sure."

Em laughed. "I wasn't even officially entered!" Everyone had to settle for the look on Em's face, which was happiness.

"Now they know," Em told Bridge. "Thanks to you, Bridge. They know that I still like myself. And they can watch me doing it all they want." This was the Em who Bridge saw on the soccer field, the one in the yellow sweatshirt who threw two fists in the air after every goal.

Then Em's face changed. "Evan!" she shouted. "Why are you here?"

Em's brother was tearing down the aisle toward them, his hands balled at his hips. He was like a very serious train, plowing right into Emily. After a couple of seconds he pulled his face out of her stomach. "You were so good."

"Who's with you? Are Mom and Dad here? But—why?" She whirled on Bridge. "Did you tell them I was singing?"

"No," Bridge said.

"Tab called last night!" Evan said. "She said I should tell Mom and Dad. We surprised you!"

271

"She did?" Emily and Bridge shared a look—of course Tab would think to call Em's parents. Who else? "Where is she?" Em scanned the room.

"There." Evan pointed. "With Celeste."

Tab and Celeste were standing together against the wall on the other side of the loud auditorium, clearly arguing.

"What's Celeste doing here?" Em said to Bridge.

"I don't know," Bridge said.

Then Emily's parents were there, hugging her, and people kept coming over to tell her how great she was. Bridge kept one hand on Evan's shoulder and watched the silent movie of Tab and Celeste. Finally they hugged, and then Tab buzzed through the crowd toward Bridge.

"Can you leave? Walk me home. I have to calm down my parents before they call the police or something."

"What's going on?"

"Total craziness. Celeste skipped school and hid out somewhere all day. My parents are freaking, even though she just talked to them twice on my phone and I keep *telling* them that she's fine. And now she says she can't go home yet! She has to do something *important,* and guess who's supposed to tap-dance for Mom and Dad until she's back? Me! The person they're already not too happy with because she got *suspended* this week!"

"You could always juggle for them," Bridge said. "I know where you can get some nice rocks."

"Don't be silly," Tab said, steering her out of the auditorium. "How am I supposed to take a bite out of a rock? Celeste said she'd meet me out front."

Outside, Tab pulled Bridge to where Celeste was standing, a little apart from the swarm of families in front of the school.

"Hey, Bridge." Celeste smiled. She was holding a red rose wrapped in cellophane and standing on one leg in an unzipped sweatshirt.

"Hey. Aren't you freezing?"

"Kind of. How was the show? Tab says Em sang. I'm sorry I missed it."

"It was actually kind of great," Bridge said.

"You sound surprised," Celeste said. "Tab, sorry to be annoying, but you have to go home right *now*. They must be climbing the walls."

"Yeah, because of you! Not me!"

"I swear I'll be there in forty-five minutes. An hour, tops."

Tab pretended to scowl. "Do *not* be late. And take my phone."

Celeste pocketed it. "Thanks." She kissed Tab and blew a kiss to Bridge. And then she turned and walked away.

They were almost to Tab's corner when Tab said, "Where are your ears?"

Bridge stopped. "My ears! I forgot all about them. They must be in the auditorium."

"Yikes, I hope they're there on Monday," Tab said.

"Yeah." But Bridge didn't miss them. She could still feel that hand on her head.

"Okay, here I go," Tab said when they reached her building. "Wish me luck."

"Good luck," Bridge said.

"Oh!" Tab yelled over her shoulder. "Happy Valentine's Day!"

That was when Bridge realized she hadn't even said good-bye to Sherm after the show. She pulled out her phone and texted him.

Bridge: Sorry I ran away! Tab emergency. ☹

Sherm: ? All okay? ☹

Bridge: Fine now.

Sherm: Where R U?

Bridge: 105th

Sherm: I'm on 106th!!

Bridge looked up and scanned the block. It was dark, but she could just make him out, standing on the corner.

Bridge: I think I see you

Sherm: I think I see you too. Can you come over?

SIX WHITE FLAGS

"I want to show you something." Sherm pulled at a latch above his head, and a trapdoor in the third-floor ceiling came down slowly until it hung in front of them like an open mouth. From this he carefully unfolded a narrow ladder that made Bridge think of a tongue reaching out to taste the floor.

"You okay with climbing?" Sherm asked. He held out a flashlight to her.

Bridge went up first, unhooking the latch on a second little door at the top and pushing it open to find herself on the roof of Sherm's house. There wasn't much open space— maybe two strides in any direction. She swung the flashlight around, though with the moon so bright she could see perfectly well without it. "Does your grandma know you come up here?"

"Yeah, she knows," Sherm called from below. "I used to go up there with my grandfather all the time. Catch!"

She caught a dark bundle that turned out to be a sleeping bag, and Sherm dragged another one behind him up the ladder. When he was standing next to her, he flipped it out in front of him and Bridge heard something go *thunk* when it hit the roof.

"Dropped my binoculars," Sherm explained.

"I'm cold," Bridge said.

They sat against the attic door with the sleeping bags pulled up to their necks. Bridge squinted into the binoculars. "I can't find it."

"What do you mean you can't find it?" Sherm said. "Keep both eyes open."

"I *am*." Then she suddenly had it. The moon.

"Wow." It glowed hugely in front of her, like something she could reach out and touch. Who knew you could see the moon like this with a regular pair of binoculars?

"Okay," Sherm said. "So you see the face, right? Look at the eye on the left, and go down a little from there. There's a dark spot."

"Yeah. I think. Yeah. Got it."

"That's the Sea of Tranquility."

"There's water up there?"

"Well, not anymore. But that's what they call it."

"Oh. 'Sea of Tranquility' sounds like it should be some-place in the Bahamas."

"That's where they landed."

"Who did?"

"Buzz Aldrin and Neil Armstrong. Apollo 11."

She lowered the binoculars and looked at Sherm. "Apollo 11? So you admit they were there?"

"First manned flight to the moon. Landed July twentieth, 1969." He shrugged. "It's a fact."

Bridge looked through the binoculars again. "What about no wind on the moon? What about the American flag?"

"The flag is still there. There are six flags up there, actually. But they're all white now. Bleached out by the sun."

"Six white flags?"

"Yeah. Like a big fat surrender."

In the moonlight, Sherm looked sad, as if he were the one surrendering. "Also, you can see their footsteps. The astronauts', I mean. The footsteps are still there in the dust, and with a really powerful telescope, you can see them from Earth."

"Wow." Bridge lowered the binoculars. "So this was kind of a grandpa thing? Something you did together, I mean."

Sherm nodded. "My grandfather is this really patriotic space-mission fan. We used to come up here a lot and he would tell me things. He actually worked at the factory that made the flag left on the moon by Apollo 11."

"Seriously?"

"The factory is in New Jersey. My dad was born right after that. That's why he's named Apollo." Sherm laughed. "Weird, right? But my grandfather used to say he had the best job in the world."

"Making flags?"

"Yep—sitting in front of a sewing machine all day. Best job in the world. That was after he got back from the war. Vietnam." Sherm reached for the binoculars. "Anyway, I wanted you to know. I was just being annoying—about the moon landing."

"Because you're mad," Bridge said. "At your grandfather."

"I guess so. Yeah."

"Like, *really* mad," Bridge said.

"Okay, thanks, Dr. Freud."

Bridge looked at the moon again. "Today's his birthday, right?"

She felt him turn to her. "How'd you know that?"

"February fourteenth. I saw it at Dollar-Eight, remember? On that piece of paper you carry around everywhere. Because your grandfather doesn't matter to you anymore."

"Shut up." He elbowed her in the dark.

"You should mail those letters."

"I'm thinking about it."

After a minute, Sherm said, "There's something I want to tell you. You're going to think I'm weird."

"I already think you're weird."

"Seriously. Be serious."

"Okay." Bridge gathered her sleeping bag around her shoulders, digging her chin into the softness of it.

"When you had your accident," Sherm said, "you were roller-skating down my block."

"Yeah, you told me. At the diner."

"But I didn't tell you that I was there. I was sitting on our steps, waiting for my dad to come out of the house. We were getting in the car to go to Chuck E. Cheese."

"Whoa. Did you actually see me get hit? Tab is, like, scarred for life from it."

"This isn't funny."

"It's *my* near-death experience—shouldn't I be allowed to joke about it?"

Sherm pointed his flashlight at his very serious face and looked at her.

"Yikes. Okay, sorry."

"My dad was the first doctor who got to you, after. He went with you in the ambulance and worked on you in surgery that night. You know he's a cardiologist, right?"

"Wow—seriously? That's crazy." Then she added, "Jamie said my heart stopped three times that night."

Sherm looked at her. "Three times?"

Bridge nodded, thinking. Sherm's *father*. "Do you realize your dad probably touched my heart? Like—directly?"

"Huh," Sherm said. "I never thought of that."

"Weird."

"My parents had to sell their car," Sherm said. "After your accident. Because I used to cry whenever I saw it. It reminded me of what happened."

"Wait." Bridge sat straight up, letting her sleeping bag slip from her shoulders. "The yellow Bug? It was double-parked?"

"You remember our *car*?"

Bridge decided not to tell him. It would only make him feel worse, and it wasn't his fault. It was nobody's fault. She sat back and closed her eyes and remembered what it had felt like, flying down the block on her skates, doing her Chaplin moves.

"Is that why you're so nice to me?" she said. "Because we have this secret connection that only you knew about?"

"Actually, I tried *not* to know you. I avoided you at school for three years. I didn't want to think about you at all."

"Nice. You watch a girl get run over and then you ignore her."

"Would you stop joking?"

"Sorry."

"Don't joke about the accident. And don't joke about—us."

Bridge was glad it was mostly dark. She didn't want to have to think about the look on her face. "Us?"

"Yes. Us."

Bridge waited. She wanted to tell Sherm about the music and how she didn't hear it yet. At least, she didn't *think* she heard it. She didn't know how to begin.

"You're my best friend," Sherm said. After a few seconds he added, "I wanted you to know."

Bridge exhaled.

"You're my best friend too," she said. "Tab, Emily, and you."

Sherm nodded, and they were quiet. Then Sherm said, "You know what my dad told me once? He said the human heart doesn't really pump the way everyone thinks."

"It doesn't?"

"No. He said that the heart wrings itself out. It twists in two different directions, like you'd do to squeeze the water out of a wet towel."

"That's pretty cool," Bridge said. She thought about her heart, wringing itself out right next to Sherm's.

They were quiet again. After a minute, Sherm said, "I'm not going to kiss you or anything."

And Bridge said, "Good."

CELESTE

That's what life is. Life is where you sleep and what you see when you wake up in the morning, and who you tell about your weird dream, and what you eat for breakfast and who you eat it with. Life isn't something that happens to you. It's something you make yourself, all the time. Life is that half minute in the morning before your cat remembers she's kind of a grouch, when she pours out her love and doesn't give a flying newton who sees it.

"A flying newton?" Gina says when you've given her the rose and spilled your guts. She smiles, but it isn't a real Gina smile.

You've just told her everything: Vinny. Your stupidity. The way you gave her secret away. The fraudulent flower for Marco.

Everything.

You're both standing in the hall next to the door of her apartment, because you told her you weren't coming in until you said what you had to say. Because after that she might not want you to come in.

"You mean like—a Fig Newton?" she says. "I don't think I get it."

"Yeah. A flying Fig Newton. From now on I'm just build-
ing my world, piece by piece, like in the apocalypse game.
No creeps allowed. And I was wondering if you still want
to be in my world, if you can be my friend, after what I did.
Because—I love you. You're a good friend, a *real* friend. And
I really want a friend like you. And I want to be one."

Gina stares at you for a second. Then she says, "That's
super. Can we go back to the part where you flat-out be-
trayed me?"

"You'll never know how sorry I am. Never."

"You're *sorry?*"

"I spent this whole day thinking about it, about *why*. I've
been a total zombie since yesterday, trying to figure out who I
am. Why I would do this."

"Wow. You spent a whole day thinking about it, huh?
After you stomped all over the most important thing in my
life? A whole *day*? You must be so wise now."

"I know it sounds stupid. And I'm not saying I have life all
figured out. All I know is that nothing like this will happen
again. I know I can be a better friend."

"Better than telling my deepest secret to a girl who is basically evil personified? Letting her humiliate me in front of
someone I love deeply and pretty much want to spend my life
with? How are you going to top that? Friend-wise, I mean?"

You want to tell her about this morning at the copy shop:
the man in the suede shirt walking away, checking his phone.
His whole life behind him, his whole life ahead of him. That's
you. That's everyone. You and Gina can choose to be friends
for life, right here and now, even if you're still learning how

to be one. Of course, she might decide to walk away instead. But you think you're probably being weird enough already, so you don't say any of that. You just say, "I don't expect you to ever really understand why I told Vinny. It's a long story. I doubt you want to hear it."

"Oh, I definitely need to hear it," Gina says.

"Really?" That gives you hope.

"You know, you aren't the first person to experience this. I had a couple of semi-evil friends, in middle school."

"You did?"

"Yeah. I have some things I could tell you too." Gina puts her hands on her hips and then slides them into her pockets. "If you want to come in."

You hug her, pinning her arms because her fists are still in her pockets. "Hey!" She laughs. "My hands are stuck!"

"I know," you tell her. "This is a one-way hug."

"Just don't knock me over."

"I won't."

The first thing Gina tells you is that Marco didn't get Vinny's flower.

"Wait a minute. So I *didn't* ruin your life?"

"Well, not *yet*."

She's pretty sure. She and Marco walked home together, and she teased him all the way about his big bunch of red carnations, and he let her read all the cards that came with them. She said he seemed like the regular Marco, beautiful and funny and completely oblivious to her feelings.

"Wow. I wonder what happened?"

"Are you sure she put the card in the box?" Gina asks. "Maybe she chickened out."

Vinny is not a chicken. But you didn't actually see the card go in. You'd stormed away from her, across the lobby, your chest full of words and hurt and helplessness. Maybe she ripped it up. Maybe she shoved the dollar back into her pocket. Maybe the Vinny you used to know isn't quite gone. If she's still in there, you thank her, silently. And say goodbye.

SHERM

February 14

Dear Nonno Gio,

   I know this is a lot of letters to get at once.

   I wasn't sure whether to send them or not, but I decided to do it. I asked Dad for your address.

   We are all fine. Write back if you want to. Or text me.

Sherm

P.S. Happy birthday.

EPILOGUE

Two Years Later

Afterward, they never agreed. They both remembered waking up that morning in the fall of ninth grade, absolutely sure. They both remembered meeting as soon as they could after school, at the top of the subway stairs, and the excitement they felt, one waiting on the sidewalk, one sprinting up the steps.

They both remembered that the Dollar-Eight Diner felt like a room full of eyes seeing them and knowing that something had changed. They both remembered thinking that it must have been obvious to anyone who bothered to look.

They both remembered deciding to stop for a minute on the way to Sherm's house, sitting together on a stoop. They both remembered being the first to reach for the other.

Bridge had always worried that it might be awful to kiss Sherm. It might be as if everything they had already been to each other wouldn't matter anymore. It might be like starting all over from nothing, like closing a book and opening another one.

But it wasn't like that. Kissing Sherm was like saying "And . . . and . . . and . . ."

Kissing Sherm didn't feel anything like the end.

ENORMOUS THANKS

to my generous and inexhaustible readers: Daphne Benedis-Grab, Judy Blundell, Kristin Cashore, Donna Freitas, Caroline Gertler, Deborah Heiligman, Randi Kish, Eli and Jack O'Brien, Deborah Stead, and Cleo Watson.

to ab-fab editor Wendy Lamb, assistant editor Dana Carey, and their thoughful readers: Sarah Eckstein, Teria Jennings, and Hannah Weverka.

to the stunning Random House team, including John Adamo, Dominique Cimina, Colleen Fellingham, Kate Gartner, Judith Haut, Casey Lloyd, Alison Kolani, Barbara Marcus, Adrienne Waintraub, and Isabel Warren-Lynch.

to my shining agent, Faye Bender.

to my friends and my family,
who show me every day what love really means.

ABOUT THE AUTHOR

Rebecca Stead is the author of three previous books for children. *When You Reach Me*, a *New York Times* bestseller, won the Newbery Medal and the *Boston Globe–Horn Book Award* for Fiction. *Liar & Spy*, also a bestseller, was named a notable book by the *New York Times Book Review* and won the *Guardian* Prize for Children's Fiction. Her first novel, *First Light*, was named a Best Book for Teens by the New York Public Library. Rebecca lives in New York City with her family.